A Christmas Hallelujah

Dori Harrell

Lindy,

Hope this brings a smile to your face!

Dori Harrell

A Christmas Hallelujah
Cranberry Creek Series, Book 1

Published by Banner Publishing

Cover Design by Lynnette Bonner, of Indie Cover Design, https://www.indiecoverdesign.com
Editing by Rachel Overton, of Wordscapes, https://www.facebook.com/WordscapesEditor/

Dori has permission from these businesses to use their names in A Christmas Hallelujah: Street Bean Coffee Roasters, Spring Harvest Fiber Mill, and Yakima Steak Company.

Scripture quotations are from the public domain King James Version of the Holy Bible.

ISBN: 978-1-948089-00-5

Printed in the USA.

Acknowledgments

I so appreciate the many people who encouraged me as I wrote and revised *A Christmas Hallelujah*. I am especially grateful to Jennifer Ely of Sage Bluff Alpacas in Prosser, Washington. Jennifer graciously gave of her time and knowledge to assure the alpaca facts were accurate. Any errors in that regard (or any other) are all mine.

A special thank-you to my nephew Raymond (nine years old at the time of publication). Raymond could not pronounce his *l*'s when the letter appeared at the beginning of a word, until he was in kindergarten. Raymond was the inspiration for Jake.

Many thanks to my husband, Doug, and Colleen Jones, Lorraine De Vries, and Denise Syverson for serving as beta readers. Your input was invaluable. And finally, a big thank-you to my wonderful editor, Rachel Overton, for her honesty, sensitivity, and cheerleading.

And God is able to make all grace abound toward you; that ye, always having all sufficiency in all things, may abound to every good work.

—2 Corinthians 9:8 KJV

Chapter 1

Piper Castleton snatched her car keys off the counter at the police station. She slid the key ring over her finger and jammed her younger sister's personal effects into her backpack—phone, lip gloss, mascara, and a crinkled photo of Dad.

Piper found it hard to believe she'd had to ride her bike to the Cranberry Creek PD to pick up her juvenile-delinquent fifteen-year-old sister, Libby. And this wasn't the first time. She ought to just leave her here and tell the officers to process her through the system since, according to the police, Libby had stolen Piper's car and blown through a stop sign—while a cop sat idling at the opposite side of the intersection. All to meet up with some friends at a coffee shop. And this wasn't the first time.

She was lucky Dad's longtime officer friend, Pete, was the cop.

As Piper perused the police station in search of Libby, she tugged off her beanie and gloves and slipped out of her fur-trimmed coat. She stuffed everything into her backpack but left it unzipped, as the jacket and hand-knit items spilled over the top. It might be near freezing outside on this November day in central Washington, but the station personnel had cranked up the thermostat. Her long-sleeved waffle-fabric henley with a thumbhole, her all-time favorite winter top, was almost too toasty. She wished she'd thought to layer.

Mom should be here handling Libby, not Piper. But since Mom had taken off two months ago to "immerse" herself in yoga so she could "connect with her psyche," Piper had been left to care for her sister on her own. And parenting a teenage girl wasn't for wimps, that was for sure.

"Where's Libby, Pete?" Piper flicked her gaze toward the cranberry-colored chairs near the counter. "There's hardly anyone sitting in the waiting area." A short distance from the seating was the door to the city's small courtroom, housed inside the police station. If Piper didn't set her sister on the straight and narrow quickly, Libby might be sitting in the defendant's box in that courtroom one of these days.

Pete, a burly guy with an auburn-and-gray flattop, stood on the other side of the counter, his elbows propped on the Formica, his features stern. "I put handcuffs on her and shoved her into one of the cells here—"

"What!" Piper might have thought jail would scare Libby straight, but she hadn't dreamed Pete would stash her sister behind bars. "Pete! Is that safe? Is she okay?"

He raised his hand. "She's by herself, no worries. But I threatened to take her to juvie, to put the fear of God into her. Juvie is not a fun place."

Piper tossed her head back to glare at the ceiling and sighed. "I appreciate the effort, truly, but because of Dad, she has no fear of the police. I'm more scared of policemen than she is, and I've never even had so much as a speeding ticket." Not that she hadn't deserved a ticket or two, but Pete didn't need to know that.

"I'll head back and let her know her cavalry has arrived."

"No! Wait. Don't tell her I'm here. Let her stew a bit longer. Act as if you're taking her to juvie. But then just haul her butt out here. I'll take it from there." Now that she knew Libby was safe, Piper's anger bubbled back to the surface.

Pete stepped from behind the counter. He placed an arm around Piper's shoulder and gave her a side hug. "I know you girls have been having a rough time of it, what with your dad gone two years now and your mom taking off like that. Libby's a good kid. She is. She's just feeling adrift right now. You're doing the best you can."

Piper sagged into Pete's gentle hug. "I'm failing her, Pete. She just wishes Mom would come home and be a mom. Me too. Libby doesn't listen to me. You know I have to drag her to church on Sundays. Mom hardly went after Dad died, and she didn't care whether Libby did or not. I don't know what to do different... And it'll be Christmas in a few weeks. Not much to celebrate around our place this year."

Pete squeezed her tight and released her. "You'll figure it out, kid. Practically the whole churchgoing part of town is praying for ya. Libby will come around. You'll see. By the way, I had a rookie drive your Jeep to the parking lot here. Hey, he's about your age—"

"Forget it. I have my hands full with Libby." And besides, she'd lost one boyfriend not long after she'd returned to Cranberry Creek to take care of her sister. They'd only been dating a few weeks, and she hadn't been serious about him, but still, it'd stung. Jefferson had been sympathetic but not even remotely interested in sticking by Piper when she'd left Spokane. The small town, a wayward teenage sister, and a missing mom didn't add up to a trifecta for Jefferson. Piper wasn't willing to risk that it wouldn't work out mathematically for any other guy either. And who knew if Mom would ever return. Maybe Piper would finish raising Libby on her own.

But one thing Piper did know—she wouldn't abandon her sister. Now, if only she could keep her out of jail.

Pete, deceptively light on his feet for such a lumbering appearance, wandered down the stark hallway and unlocked the steel door leading to the mysterious back area, a space Piper had never seen and hoped Libby would never see again.

Piper headed to the waiting area and spotted a chair with duct tape holding its faux-leather seat together. At least someone had tried to match the deep-red color. The police department was located in a remodeled former fruit warehouse, and the city usually prided itself on how well it kept up its historical buildings. The reception and office areas behind the Plexiglas panes even contained the original but now restored wide-plank wood flooring, though olive Berber covered the rest of the areas. She was sure the station would get around to having this seat reupholstered, but in the meantime, she'd do her part to protect the city's image by covering up the duct tape with her bottom.

She slipped the backpack off and set it by her feet. Her elbows landed on her knees and her forehead on her palms. She flicked her ponytail behind her when it draped over her shoulder. She offered up a silent prayer, though a wide chasm existed between her and God at the moment. She just didn't understand why He would have allowed their mother to walk out on her teenage daughter. And what did Piper know about parenting a teen girl? But even great parents of teens sometimes found themselves in police stations praying for God's intervention, she supposed.

Lord, please show me what it'll take to help Libby through the loss of our only parent left. Dad's death was easier on her than Mom's rejection. Please...

She wished Pete would hurry out with Libby. Time to sit meant time to think, and her thoughts coasted to Mom's fateful call.

Piper had been illustrating full time for Kiddles, a Spokane-based publisher of kids' literature, her dream job. And she had just released her own children's book. Mom's out-of-the-blue mandate that Piper hurry home to the alpaca ranch had punctured her immediate dreams, but Mom flying off to who knew where had shattered Libby's fragile heart.

Piper knew her sister was acting out in response to the trauma, but she didn't know how to best help her gain some equilibrium. She argued constantly, which drove Piper crazy. Libby had even snuck out once to hang out with kids who'd raided their parents' liquor cabinets, which had ended in her first official visit to the Cranberry Creek PD.

Thanksgiving was next week. Libby had already said she wanted to skip the holiday this year, and Piper had agreed. Her sister would likely say the same thing about Christmas, but Piper already had a plan in motion. Somehow she'd find a way to make Christmas less melancholy for Libby, for herself.

What was taking Pete so long anyway? It wasn't as if Libby had been arrested. At least, he hadn't said he'd formally charged her. Had he? Piper twirled her ponytail in a tight swirl and released it, repeatedly, trying to recall if Pete had actually used the word *arrest.*

He wouldn't bring Libby out in handcuffs, would he?

She craned her neck toward the hallway and slumped in relief when she saw Libby's blond hair and lithe five-foot-seven form—a good three inches taller than her older sister, much to Piper's chagrin—round the hallway corner, her handcuff-free hands stuffed into the pockets of her torn-at-the-knees skinny jeans. Her oversized unzipped sweatshirt drooped off one shoulder, revealing a white tank top underneath. Libby wore tank tops every day, spring, summer, fall, or winter.

Pete strolled right behind Libby. He placed a hand on her back, as if urging her forward.

Piper left her backpack on the floor and sprinted toward her sister, enveloping her in a tight hug, rocking her back and forth, until the single calm brain cell she'd crammed her anger into split open, an atom about to go nuclear. She broke the hug to hold her sister at arm's length.

"Girl, no phone, no tablet, and you are so not getting Ding Dongs for a week!"

"OMG, Piper—"

Piper thumped her on the arm.

"Okay, okay. Sorry. No taking the Lord's name in vain. I know. But everyone says it."

Piper tilted her head and narrowed her eyes.

"I said I was sorry. But you're overreacting! You're taking my phone and tablet and sending me to Ding Dong jail? That's worse than where I just was..."

Piper's point exactly.

"You're such a buzzkill. Can't you just spank me and send me to bed without dinner? It's not like I'd be missing much. I'm tired of that whole-food crap you always buy anyway."

Piper slugged Libby's other arm, then pulled her toward her again for a quick embrace before turning to hug Pete. "Thanks for keeping her safe, Pete."

"You're welcome. But, Libby, you've been brought in for underage drinking and now for driving without a license. These might seem like small offenses, but they aren't. You've gotten a couple lucky breaks because of your dad's twenty years on the force here, but if you mess up again, the third time won't be a charm. We got a couple new guys who didn't know Paul Castleton, and they won't care one whit about his little girl."

Piper cocked her head toward Libby. "D'you hear that?"

Libby didn't even have the grace to look at the floor in contrition. "Someone's got to keep you guys on your toes, Pete."

"Let's leave that to someone else's baby sister," Piper said. She waved to Pete while she tugged Libby toward her backpack. "We'll talk more at the ranch. We have a ton of work to do, girl. Here, take my coat and give me your sweatshirt. You'll want my beanie and gloves too. I've knit you so many hats. It's so cold out. You'd think you could wear one. You're lucky it's not snowing."

"You sound so much like Mom."

Piper froze, her arm stretched out, the jacket dangling from her fingers.

Libby crossed her arms over her chest and dipped her chin down, her curtain of shoulder-length hair shielding her face. She finally lifted her gaze and stared at the knitted accessories Piper had draped over the duct-taped chair.

"Why am I lucky it's not snowing? I love snow! What's wrong with my sweatshirt anyway? If it's good enough for you, it's good enough for me."

"Oh, you're definitely going to want my coat and hat and gloves when you ride my bike home." She tipped her head and looked squarely into the stormy waves of her sister's baby blues, so unlike Piper's plain brown eyes. Libby had been on the receiving end of their mom's blond blue-eyed Dutch ancestors.

Piper took after her dad's redheaded, pointy-chinned English-Irish side. The short end of the stick, in her opinion.

"How did you think I got here so quickly? You stole my car! Which of course means I'll be hiding my keys from now on. We live in the country, Libby. Hello! It would have taken me more than an hour to walk here, and both neighbors were gone. So I rode my bike. It's locked to a signpost outside. And you'll be riding it back to the ranch."

"I'm not riding that old thing! It still has a basket on the handlebars. You can't do this to me. What if someone sees me? I'll do anything. Not that."

"Take off your sweatshirt, Libby."

Libby sighed and slipped her sweatshirt off her shoulders. "I should at least get one Ding Dong this week! Two if somebody sees me."

Piper forced her green jacket into Libby's hand. That girl and her chocolate. She'd eat those silly give-her-a-sugar-high confections for breakfast, lunch, and dinner. "They're in the safe." Which Libby didn't have the combo to. "Maybe next time you'll ride your bike to the coffee shop to meet your friends on a Saturday. Couldn't you have waited till I got back from my run? Did you even check on Sophia before you took off?" Their prized alpaca dam was just a few weeks from delivering twins.

"Sophia's fine. You run for a ridiculous two hours on Saturdays! Chloe's mom wouldn't come and get me. I'd've made it home before you got back if it hadn't been for Pete."

"Those long runs help keep me sane. And really, Libby? You're blaming Pete?"

She shoved the hat at her sister, who snugged it over her enviably straight locks.

"Now hustle up, girl. I want to check on Sophia. And don't

even think about not wearing the bike helmet. It fits over that hat, and it's in the basket."

Chapter 2

"Dad, stop! Alpaca, alpaca."

"Jake, you can't just scream at me while I'm driving," Alex said as he turned a sharp left and skidded the Dakota pickup into the driveway beside which stood a sign announcing *Cranberry Creek Criations, an Alpaca Ranch.* Sure enough, the straw-strewn gravel edged a spacious winter-brown lawn that fronted a low wooden rail with a wire-woven fence directly behind. Two alpacas stood with their heads bent over the palm of a copper-haired, ponytailed girl. Was she talking to them?

"Just wike in my book." Jake chattered from his car seat in the back. "Can we get out? I wanna see the alpacas and..."

The girl straightened and pressed against the wire fence, looking their direction. Even from the driveway, Alex could see the redhead was no *girl.* The alpaca on her left clearly missed her attention, and the woman held out her palm to it.

Piper? They'd get out all right, but not just to see the fluffy creatures.

Alex's chest tightened as attraction zinged through him. He leaned his forehead against the steering wheel. He hadn't looked twice at another woman since Amy died a year and a half ago.

Why such a strong reaction to Piper? It wasn't as if he'd been close to her. She was a few years younger. He'd only seen her a handful of times at church when he'd vacationed with his parents at their Cranberry Creek cabin, and he hadn't been back since his sophomore year in high school. He had no special weakness for redheads, though that might be changing. Piper's obvious poignant connection with those alpacas stirred something in him. Something he had to ignore.

With his almost-four-year-old son attached to his side 24/7, Alex couldn't entertain even the notion of a romantic relationship.

"Dad, I can't get my buckle off." Jake jabbed his feet into the back of Alex's seat.

If Alex had only been five eleven instead of six feet, he wouldn't have had to adjust the seat back far enough that Jake could reach it with his feet.

Alex stepped out of the car as Piper opened a gate. His gaze took in her—

"Dad! What's taking you so wong?"

He opened Jake's door and clicked the stubborn buckle. His son slid the straps off and leaped onto the gravel, righting himself after a wobbly landing.

Jake grabbed Alex's hand. "Is Mikko here? He's my fav'rit'."

Alex grinned down at Jake. "Hang on, buddy. We have to ask permission first."

"Can we ask the wady with red hair?"

Alex glanced up into Piper's huge deep-chocolate eyes looking at him questioningly.

He didn't have any special attraction to chocolate either. Or freckles.

It wasn't every day a gorgeous sandy-haired stranger

landed on her ranch, and Piper crouched till one knee rested on the ground so she could look this cutie pie in his hazel eyes.

She smiled and held out her hand. "Welcome to Criations. We love kids here. I'm Piper. What's your name?"

After a morning like she'd had, she welcomed the diversion of two eye-catching males on her property.

The boy looked up at the man, just a tad less good looking than his son, if she'd assessed the relationship right. Wait. Was that...Alex Saunders? With broader shoulders and scruff on his jaw. Not too many guys had that dimple in their chins. But he hadn't been around Cranberry Creek in years. She'd heard he'd married and started some company over in Seattle. And that his wife had passed away.

"Go ahead, Jake," the man said.

The little boy stretched a tentative right hand toward Piper even as he gripped the man's fingers tighter.

"Do Mikko and Pikko wive here?"

Apparently they were going to skip the introduction and get right to the heart of the meeting. Piper preferred directness, so that suited her just fine. She gripped Jake's hand in hers and gave it a quick shake, his little fingers still warm, but they'd cool rapidly on this forty-degree day, even with the sunshine.

"You must have read my book! But in real life, Mikko and Pikko are still in their mommy's tummy," Piper said, delighted to hear her children's story, *Mikko and Pikko Rock the Ranch*, had actually been read to a young child. "Fresca and Dominique live here though."

He glanced up at the man. "They're not in my book, Daddy."

"Fresca and Dominique will be Mikko and Pikko's friends one day. When the mama, Sophia, has her babies next month—we call them *crias*—I plan to name them Mikko and Pikko, just like in the book." She deliberately didn't mention that one cria usually didn't survive and that raising alpaca twins was a rarity. She'd written the book about twin alpacas in hopes that Sophia's birth would produce two surviving crias.

Piper wanted to look up at the guy she thought was Alex, but she could hardly take her eyes off his adorable son.

She rose though and curved her lips upward. Her smile probably looked lopsided or something. A morning spent at the police station would wipe the mirth off anyone's expression.

But this guy with the cute son didn't know all that. Hopefully, he thought her smile looked normal. Maybe even nice. At least her teeth were white and not smeared with lipstick. She'd given up lipstick since moving back to the ranch.

Jake's father had light-brown wavy hair and the same hazel eyes as his son. Did she detect a hint of sadness in them? Or was she just overly sensitive right now? She clasped the warm, strong, uncalloused palm he had extended, noting again the breadth of shoulders underneath his fleece Seahawks jacket. Her pulse skittered in an unfamiliar beat that made her dizzy.

Must be the cold air settling in. She still wore only Libby's sweatshirt over her henley.

"Hi, Piper. Do you remember me? Alex Saunders. We saw each other at church a few times growing up, when I was in town with my parents. This little guy is Jake, and I'm the lucky one who gets to be his dad."

What a great introduction—Piper might try that next time. *This rebel teen is Libby, and I'm the unlucky one who gets to be her sister.* What? She hadn't meant that. It came out wrong in her mind.

Did she have to let Alex's fingers go? She supposed so.

"Jake saw your book at the bookstore, in the local-author section," Alex said, "and we bought it. He's entranced with it."

Alex's grin converted his handsome face into extraordinary looking, nearly outshining his son's. Piper placed a hand on her jittery stomach. Her insides had never reacted to Alex like that before. Of course, she'd been in...what? The seventh or eighth grade the last time she'd seen him?

"I am guilty of looking you up on Google and trying to find your ranch, based on your author bio. And Jake was beyond excited that he might meet Mikko and Pikko. I hope you don't mind."

"Not at all! I'm glad you liked the book, Jake. I had so much fun writing and illustrating it." Kiddles had worked with her in creating her book. When she'd had to leave Spokane, they allowed her to freelance illustrate for them from the ranch.

And at least one kid loved her book!

Piper motioned toward the fence. "Would you gentlemen like to meet Fresca and Dominique? They're in the display area right now." She rotated on the ball of her foot and led them through a gate. "They're quite kid friendly."

Piper dipped her hand into her grain baggie and held a flat palm out to Dominique, a ginger-colored creature, as Fresca, a white and brown pinto, jutted her head in.

"Jake, would you like to feed Dominque some grain?" Piper asked. "She likes it best if you reach out your hand slowly."

Piper deposited a few grain kibbles into Jake's palm, and he tipped forward ever so slightly.

"Can I pet her?"

"No, the alpacas prefer not to be touched at all. They'll let you show affection other ways though. I'll show you in a minute."

"Will she bite me?" He halted the hand that had been

headed toward Dominique. "She wooks wike she's smiling. Does that mean she wikes me?"

"She won't bite you. She's super friendly. But if you move your hand too fast, she might take off to have a snack of hay in the corner over there."

Jake tentatively unbent his elbow.

"Daddy, it doesn't hurt. She's soft!"

Alex's eyes crinkled when he stared at his son, again with that hint of sadness that snagged Piper's heart. Because of her own circumstances, she was probably more attuned to someone else's emotions.

Fresca clearly felt left out, so Piper handed Jake some more kibbles and pushed his arm her way.

"Can I ride her?" he asked.

Piper laughed what felt like her first genuine laugh in two months. That had to be the most-often-asked question by a child. "If she were a horse, you could ride her. But she's an alpaca, and you would hurt her if you rode her. Besides, she'd probably buck you off and spit at you. Yuck!"

"Eww..." Jake jerked back his hand, startling Dominique, who trotted backward several steps.

Alex grasped his son's hand. "Hey, buddy, I think we should head—"

"Next time you can ride your own da—darn bike home!"

Oh no! Piper pivoted at the sound of Libby's voice.

"Next time, don't steal my car!" Had she said that out loud? She peeked at Alex and Jake as Libby pedaled toward the fence, hopped off the bike, and let it crash to the ground.

Chapter 3

Alex grasped Jake's hand and followed Piper into the yard. The genuine liking she'd taken to Jake spread a warmth through Alex he hadn't felt since...since he couldn't remember when. But he couldn't possibly think of another woman so soon after Amy, and Jake's separation anxiety should be enough to squelch even a hint of attraction. It would be such a serious complication to even the thought of a relationship.

Besides, the cute redhead—much prettier than he remembered—who'd charmed his son and, yes, himself, was dealing with her own drama. He'd had enough drama to last him a lifetime. Two lifetimes. A shudder rippled his spine as the sullen blond-haired teen yanked off her bike helmet and knit cap, tossed them on the grass, and marched up to Piper, her glare twin blue embers.

She couldn't possibly be Piper's daughter. Maybe her little sister? But...she stole a car? Huh?

"Maybe I could push Jake on the tire swing..." Alex nudged Jake toward the chestnut tree in the side yard, but his son stood his ground, staring at the teenager.

"It's only four or five miles, Libby. Don't be such a baby." Piper strode the few feet to the old pink Schwinn. She set it up on its kickstand. "And if you hadn't—"

"I so get a Ding Dong. And my phone back. Bodie Jackson saw me! What if he took a video? It'll be all over Snapchat. I'll never be able to face my friends again. My life is so over!" The teen whirled around and stalked past Jake and Alex.

She halted midstride and then walked backward till she faced Jake. She didn't apologize or fidget. She just tipped her head toward Piper.

The redhead sighed. "Jake, this is my little sister, Libby. Your dad might remember her."

"Hey…" Libby tapped her lips as she pondered Alex. "I kind of remember you. Wow. We haven't seen you in years. We see your parents at church though."

"It's been great to be back."

"Alex read my book to Jake, who wanted to meet Mikko and Pikko." Piper directed a smile at Jake.

But his son had eyes only for Piper's sister. Wasn't she cold in those ripped-up jeans?

"Somebody here read your book!" Libby beamed at Piper, the blonde's angst disappearing like mist into the sun-draped chilly air.

When she lost the scowl, her face transformed into pretty.

"That's so cool, sis."

She knelt in front of Jake, much as Piper had done earlier. "Hey, Jake. Did you get to feed Fresca and Dominique?"

Jake backed into Alex's legs. "Yes, but I really want to see Mikko and Pikko from the book. 'Specially Mikko. He's the funny one."

"I can kind of show them to you. They're in their mommy's tummy. You want to meet their mommy, Sophia? That'll be kind of like meeting them. And I bet Sophia will give you a kiss. I'll show you what to do for that."

She grabbed the grain bag from Piper as she moved her other hand toward Jake. She didn't even look up at Alex for permission. The kid obviously knew her way around the ranch. But no way would Jake take off with her.

His son placed a tentative hand into Libby's but didn't let go of Alex.

"Is she far away? Will you come, Dad?"

"We don't need your dad," Libby said. "Let him stay and talk to my boring sister. It'll just be us kids. Sophia's right over there by that paddock. We call that the maternity area. It's for mommies who have babies in their tummies." Libby pointed behind her. "You'll be able to see your dad the whole time."

"I'm sorry," Alex said, "but Jake won't—"

"Daddy, you stay right here. Don't weave. Just stay right here by Piper." Jake's eyes pleaded along with his voice.

Alex stared at his son, his jaw open. He clicked it shut as his throat contracted in disbelief. Was this blond teenager some kind of sorceress? He couldn't swallow the lump of emotion. It would make his voice husky, but he didn't care...though he'd rather it be Sam Elliott husky than Optimus Prime husky.

"I won't move, buddy. I promise. I'll stay right here where you can see me."

Was Alex going to cry? Why didn't he want Jake to go with Libby? Was there something wrong with the boy? For all Libby's teenage brattiness, she adored children and had the sweetest side to her. And for whatever reason, this kid who sometimes couldn't pronounce his *l*'s coaxed it out of her. Hopefully, it would last.

Piper pulled her cold hand from her pocket and lightly touched Alex's arm. She jumped as a zap adhered her fingers to his bicep. *What they say about electric jolts is true.* She stared at her electrocuted fingers. She hadn't felt that zing when she'd shaken his hand. Static electricity maybe? The dizziness returned. She shivered. *Cold weather doesn't usually affect me like this.*

Alex twitched and glanced down at his arm. Had he felt it? She yanked her hand back and flexed her tingly fingers.

"Do you want to follow them?" Piper asked.

He tilted his head her direction, and she noted surprise and poignancy in his expression. He opened his mouth to say something, but no words emerged. He staggered to the wooden fence and leaned hard against it.

"I think your sister has cast a spell on Jake." One side of his mouth edged up, and he sucked in a deep breath. "Ever since his mom...passed away, that boy hasn't left my side for a second. He certainly doesn't wander away with someone he doesn't know. I've never seen him walk that far away from me when we're not home. Not to go to Sunday school, not at a park. Not even to my mom. But I need to stay in his line of sight. If he can't see me, he'll freak."

Piper braced a hip against the fence, angling her body so she faced him. She was glad her dad hadn't torn down the wooden rail before he'd installed the woven wire behind it. It supported Alex's weight as turmoil punctuated his features. There must be a lot more to the story, and she might never hear it, but this one good deed of her sister's almost made up for her delinquency this morning. Maybe she could have half a Ding Dong. But still no phone.

"It's okay," Piper said softly. "My sister will have picked

up on that. She'll keep Jake where he can see you, and you're welcome to join them by Sophia."

Alex shook his head. "No way am I going spoil this moment for him or me. Hopefully, as long as he can see me, he'll be fine." He locked his dreamy hazel eyes right to hers. "You're the first person I've talked to alone—well, sort of alone—in over a year."

Piper held back the many questions filtering through her mind. Had the mom's death traumatized the boy? How did Alex manage his company? What about bedtime?

A peek in Jake's direction revealed he swiveled his head every few seconds to make sure his dad stayed put.

Libby had taken the boy inside the paddock, where Sophia and Jasmine and a couple others scurried over for treats. Libby bent at the knees, dropped her hands to her sides, and tipped forward, demonstrating the position Jake should take for an alpaca kiss. He copied her movements, and Sophia lowered her nose.

"You might want to watch this." Piper gestured toward the paddock.

Alex twisted that direction just as Sophia's nose touched Jake's face.

"Dad, she kissed me!" Jake yelled.

"That's great, buddy!"

Piper shivered again, wishing she'd sent Libby inside to get her own coat. Out of sheer habit, Piper had gone straight to greet Fresca and Dominique when she'd returned to Criations from the police station. Those two had scampered for the fence the minute the Jeep rolled into the driveway. And Alex had pulled in within minutes of that.

She tweaked her ponytail when she thought of Libby's

entry onto their property. "I'm sorry for the fuss when Libby rode in." No way would she tell him about the police station.

"She stole your car?" His left eyebrow quirked.

Piper snorted and began what she'd intended to be the short version of today's trip to Cranberry Creek PD, but found herself ending with, "Our mom took off to a yoga camp in Hawaii to find herself a couple months ago, and I left Spokane to take care of Libby and manage the ranch. Libby's devastated. She's been acting out ever since. I'm praying...I'm praying I can somehow, someway, pull her back from the edge. I'm eight years older than she is, but it's hard for her to view me as an authority figure. And frankly, it's hard to be her authority figure."

Piper clamped her lips. He was practically a stranger. But he'd shared something intimate with her, and he didn't *feel* like a stranger, since she'd kind of known him as kid. It wasn't like the whole town didn't already know about Mom.

But he wasn't from around here, and maybe he hadn't heard. Her gaze explored his pricey jeans, trendy knit scarf, and brown loafers. More the urban west side of the Cascades, the mountain range dividing Washington in half, than the semirural east side of the state.

He rotated those expansive shoulders toward the paddock again. Piper doubted he was aware he followed Jake's movements almost as much as Jake tracked him.

The first time he'd been semi-alone with a woman in a year, and she couldn't keep his attention for more than a couple of minutes. This day just kept getting more pathetic.

Not that she wanted to chat with a good-looking guy, right? Especially one from the west side of the state. Even if he did have a cute son.

And who'd want to hear more about her crazy life anyway?

"So you like living on the brown, sagebrush, tumbleweed side of the state?"

Apparently Alex did, that was who.

"Jake seems just fine over there with Libby," he said as he swung around to face her, his back to his son for the first time, one loafered foot pressing into the bottom rail, his right hand firm on the top board.

Was he challenging her with that tumbleweed comment? She dealt with an argumentative teenager every day. No way could he best Piper. She hoisted herself up so she sat on the top rail.

"You mean the sunny, blue sky—look up, dude—and arid side of the state? Yeah, I do. And proud of it! So you like living on the wet and drizzly side of the state?" She screwed her face into a grimace.

"You mean the emerald and ocean-blue and views-of-Rainier side? What's not to love about that?"

Piper raised her arms high and trickled her fingers downward till they passed in front of his face. "Maybe that it rains all day, every day."

"Not usually all day." He laughed. "But you've got me there."

"So, you like hot, fresh-mulled cider?"

"Yeah. You got a problem with that too?"

"No! We agree on something." Feeling brave considering the trauma to her fingers the last time she'd touched him, Piper placed a hand on his shoulder and thrust herself off the fence.

"Our neighbors have a cider press, so when I say fresh, I mean fresh. It'll only take me a second to heat it up."

"That'd be great," Alex said. "Jake, I think, would love a cup too. Apple juice is his favorite."

"Tree Top is headquartered right here in the Yakima Valley, in Selah. Another point for the east side. Score!" She pushed a fist forward.

He ignored it rather than fist bump it.

"Okay then." She jogged backward a few steps, hoping she wouldn't trip and fall on her rump. "I'll bring it out in a few. It's chilly today, even with all this sunshine." She smirked. "But we might get our first snowfall in a couple of weeks. Oh yeah. We get beautiful, fluffy snow here too."

"You'd better, or Jake will be devastated. He's too young to remember the one time he saw snow in Seattle. He's been praying every day for snow since we arrived at my parents' cabin a couple weeks ago."

"He and Libby both! That girl *loves* snow." She twirled. "I'll be back in a jiffy with the cider."

She prayed the whole way to the house. *Please, God. No more disasters today. Help Libby behave herself at least until Alex and Jake leave.*

Alex plopped down onto the twin bed in his and Jake's room at his parents' cedar cabin. He slid Jake's Transformer T-shirt up over his head and replaced it with his Transformer pajama top. Jake loved everything Transformer, and Bumble Bee and Optimus Prime sat at the end of his race-car bed. Even though the cabin had three other empty bedrooms, Alex's double bed was on the other side of the nightstand so that when Jake opened his eyes in the morning, he could see his dad.

Thank goodness the room was huge. It kept the two of them from becoming claustrophobic, like at their small Belltown condo. His mom had decorated the windowsills with mini pumpkins and electric candles, which Jake insisted be left on till he fell asleep.

"Know what I think, Daddy?" Jake said as he stepped out of his jeans and kicked them away. "I think Wibby wants me to come back to see Sophia. She said I could see her anytime."

Ever since they'd arrived home, it was "Wibby" this and "Sophia" that and the "twin crias in her tummy." The whole ranch experience had enchanted his son, who'd never even been to a petting zoo. Who knew he'd take to animals like that?

Of course, Alex wouldn't mind a return trip either. Not to see the alpacas though. But he should probably stay away from that attractive redhead, for both their sakes. Between Jake's separation anxiety and Piper's troubled sister, the last thing either he or Piper needed was more drama. A moment of pique tweaked his thoughts. Libby had invited Jake back, but Piper hadn't made the same suggestion to Alex. The four had enjoyed the mulled cider under the chestnut tree while Jake chatted about Mikko and Pikko being ready to be "borned," and then Piper had given Libby a list of chores and said something about needing to head to town to meet a friend. She distinctly had not suggested that Alex return. Why not? Didn't she like his dimple?

Why didn't I invite her for coffee or something? Because the thought never occurred to him, that was why. He'd never be able to have even a cup of coffee with just her. Then again, Jake did love coffeehouses... Sometimes, when Alex needed a break from working at the office or home, he'd load Jake into the Audi and head to a cozy espresso bar. Jake would order sugar disguised as a strawberry and whipped-cream drink and then color or play with his Transformers or dinosaurs while Alex contemplated a new app to design. Alex wouldn't mind meeting Piper at a coffee shop.

And if she brought Libby, the sister could distract Jake so Alex could focus on Piper.

He shook his head. What was it about her? Her heart-shaped face? Gamine smile? Freckles? Snappy wit? What? He couldn't recall ever feeling so immediately attracted to a woman, not even Amy. Guilt edged forward, but he shoved it back into its box. They'd made their mistakes, and getting pregnant and married in the wrong order was only one of them. None of that had anything to do with Piper.

How could he go so quickly from one extreme to the other over the alpaca rancher?

Stay away from her...see her again...keep his distance... return to the ranch.

"Do you think you can find an alpaca Transformer for me?"

"I don't think so, buddy. I think you have every single one there is," Alex said as he handed Jake his dirty clothes. Jake started toward the door, then turned to see if Alex was coming.

Alex picked up his own items, and together they walked to the laundry room. If he hadn't, Jake would have simply stopped and waited for him. He'd been diagnosed with severe separation anxiety disorder nine months after Amy's death.

For the umpteenth time, Alex pondered how much Amy had changed after Jake was born. She'd become fearful, never letting him out of her sight. Wanting to do the same with Alex. Jake had not spent one minute away from his mother when an infection claimed her young life.

I can design an app to solve almost any problem, he thought as he watched Jake toss his clothes into the hamper. *Tracking a teenager, the fastest commute to and from the office, even the perfect hair color. But not this.* He couldn't design something to keep his son from panicking. Jake's pediatrician had thought Jake would outgrow it, but he hadn't. After the holidays and once back in Seattle, Alex planned to contact a therapist. He and Jake couldn't go on like this much longer.

Not if he wanted to pursue a certain redhead. Which he couldn't. Not now. But if he did—

"...And Mikko could play with me when he's borned."

Jake's chatter snapped Alex's attention back to his son.

"When he's born."

Alex only corrected Jake when he used bad grammar. He had been instructed by Jake's doctor to stop correcting him when he mispronounced his *l* words. Apparently, most minor speech issues cleared up before a child turned six. However, Alex still found himself itching to insist Jake say Libby's name with an *L*.

Alex patted his son on his bottom. "If you want Grandma to read you a bedtime story, you'd better get to the family room." He hunched down. "And you know we don't live in Cranberry Creek, right? We're only staying with Papa and Grandma for the holidays."

"I know we wive in Seattle. I'm not a baby," Jake said. "But Wibby said *anytime*."

The girl couldn't be all that bad.

To think, if it hadn't been for his son, he'd have skipped the holidays this year. But his wise mom, whom he should have listened to more often in his life, had insisted he and Jake step out of the comfort zone of their condo and Alex's office and come for an extended visit. She and Dad had even threatened to drive to Seattle and drag Alex and Jake to the cabin.

Thank God for moms.

Chapter 4

Piper banged on Libby's door on Sunday morning. "Hey! Get your butt out here and help me take care of the animals before church!" Piper cringed at her own words. Her sister was supposed to have set her alarm and be up already, but she wasn't. Frustrated, Piper found herself demanding rather than enticing. Maybe she'd try a little bribe instead.

"Look...baby. If you'll come and help me with the alpacas, I'll take you to Java Creek this morning before church." Piper had been calling her *baby* since Libby had been born. She'd also already arranged to meet her friend Callie at the coffee shop, but Libby didn't know that.

"I want a Ding Dong too!"

The reply was instantaneous and not even in a sleepy voice. The girl was wide awake. But not on her phone or tablet. Piper had those locked in the safe too, along with the chocolate. Was Libby just lying there or what?

"You're not getting Ding Dongs for a week!"

"I want a coconut-milk mocha-caramel macchiato with extra whip and a scone then."

Piper opened the door and peeked her head into the room, her hands gripping the door's edge. "Deal. But just because I'm such a good sister. You know you have to get up and help me with the animals anyway." Her gaze skimmed the clothes-spattered room. She'd long given up on insisting Libby keep it clean. "What're you doing?"

"Just chillin'. Mom always let me sleep in on Sundays and just did the ranch work herself." Libby pushed herself into a sitting position, her turquoise chenille bedspread falling to her waist. She rubbed her eyes, just as she'd done when she'd been little.

Piper's heart stirred. She could see why Libby always got away with murder. The girl could be sweet and ooze charm when she wanted to. Mom had spoiled her terribly, and Piper felt an inclination to do the same sometimes. Which she instantly quelled. Libby would become more unbearable.

If they wanted to keep the ranch, they would have to work it together. It was all they had left besides each other, and no way would Piper risk losing it. On top of that, Libby adored the alpacas, and they her. Piper knew Libby didn't really mind helping most of the time. She put up a fuss more out of a teenage obligation to do so.

Piper pattered to the bed and sat on the edge, pulling Libby into a half hug. "Little sister, as you so often point out to me, I'm not your mother. It'll take me twice as long without you, and I might not finish in time for church. We have to layer the straw in the shelters. And it's below freezing, so we have to check for frozen water."

Libby leaned into Piper and put her head on her shoulder. "I miss Mom. Did she text you this morning?"

Piper set her chin on Libby's head. "I miss her too. And yeah. I received her text. She loves us. It's hot in Hawaii. Blah blah blah. Nothing new."

"Do you think she'll ever come back?"

Piper shook her head. "I don't know. She just sort of fell apart when Dad died. She can't seem to center herself anymore. And not going to church doesn't help that."

Mom texted Piper most Sunday mornings. Two lines, almost the same, every week. When Mom had first taken off, Libby had refused to reply to any of her texts, but though she'd never admit it, she'd lived to receive them. Watching Libby spiral downward emotionally with every message that didn't announce Mom's return had broken Piper's heart, so she'd texted Mom to stop sending Libby messages.

How their mother could dismiss a daughter like Libby from her life baffled Piper. She'd been out of college and on her own and settled in a job she loved when she'd received that call from Mom. But Libby, she still needed her mother.

Piper's sister sat up straight and swung her legs over the edge of the bed. Conversation over. Beyond asking if Mom would return, Libby refused to talk about her. Piper ached to heal the hurt and soothe the pain, but Libby's acting out had created a tension barrier that Piper had no idea how to breach. And as hard as she tried, she couldn't ever fill the gaping hole in Libby's heart. The one thing she could do was be there for her. Even when she didn't want to be. Like, having to show up at police stations.

"Missing church doesn't sound like a terrible idea."

"Not today, Libby. Please don't start." Piper flung herself backward onto Libby's pillow. She just couldn't deal with this today.

"That Alex was cute yesterday, huh?" Libby stood and stretched, tilting her lips in a smirk.

Where did that come from? It was so random. So out of the blue. So typical Libby.

"His son is certainly a little charmer."

"OMG, yes." At Piper's glare, she lifted her hands to her shoulders, palms up. "Sorry. But that kid. He's so adorable. He just kept talking about your book and Mikko and Pikko. But his dad. He was so..." Libby fanned her face with her hand.

Piper slapped Libby on the bottom. "Better wear a flannel shirt this morning."

"You're so not getting out of this." Libby tugged on her boyfriend-style jeans over her pajama shorts and grabbed a quilted flannel button-down off the floor. "I saw how you two looked at each other you while we were drinking that cider yesterday."

"Uh, Libby, people look at each other when they're having conversations," Piper said to her sister's back.

Libby knelt beside the bed and tucked her head near the floor. Reaching under the frame, she pulled out a work boot. "Do you see my other boot anywhere? It's not under here."

Piper scanned the room and then hopped off the mattress to grab the other boot from in front of the closet, underneath a pair of jeans and a tank top, and handed it to her sister.

"No way, sis. That wasn't just conversation. You two were *looking* at each other." Libby sat on the cedar chest at the end of her bed and laced up her boots.

Piper sat beside Libby and finger combed her sister's silky tresses. "I told you—keep those boots in the mudroom. They're icky. And Alex and I were just making friendly conversation. I'm not interested in the guy. He has a son and lives in Seattle. And he seems to like it there. Can you believe it? Anyway, I can barely handle my own life. A relationship seems too complicated right now. And a long-distance one... We know how my last attempt turned out."

"Oh, but you've thought it through, haven't you?" Libby stood to her full height and flanked her hips with her fingers. "That Jefferson was cute, but he was a wimp with a capital W. 'You need to get a handle on that girl, Piper,'" she said, her voice low and squeaky.

She mimicked Jefferson well.

"I'm not sorry he broke up with you. He talked like I wasn't in the room. When Alex talks, he looks you in the eyes."

Piper launched to her feet and lightly shoved her sister toward the door. "Girl, I told you how amazed Alex was, and so grateful for what you did for Jake"—Piper sputtered as her throat thickened—"but he barely spoke two words to you beyond 'thank you.'"

"That's because he was too busy ogling you," Libby said, glancing back as she clomped down the hallway to the family room.

Piper grabbed her jacket and followed her to the fence outside. "Get the herding wands and let the mommies and babies into the pasture. After that, layer the shelters with straw, and I'll take care of refilling the water bowls. If you finish before me, go make sure Sophia is okay and break up a hay bale in maternity. And sprinkle her herbs onto her grain." Piper had concocted an herb mixture that helped expectant mamas to lactate. A common problem with twin crias was that the mother couldn't produce enough milk, so she was being extra vigilant with Sophia.

"On it, sis." Libby flung open the gate and took off in a lope toward the laneway to the paddocks but stopped after a few steps and shouted, "Thanks for giving me the easy jobs!"

Libby didn't smile often these days. But Piper felt the grin in her words. Libby had smiled at Jake a couple of times yesterday too, and Piper thanked God for the gift of that little boy's visit.

And that of the attractive father who left her all tingly—her insides prickled at the thought of him.

She filled two five-gallon buckets with warm water from the industrial sink in the barn, plunked them onto the carrier on the back of the four-wheel Honda ATV, and drove to the laneway. But her mind was hardly focused on her task.

Seeing Alex choke up over his boy with Libby had rendered Piper's insides to mush. She assured herself that it was a normal reaction and didn't mean she was seriously attracted to the good-looking single dad Libby described as "so hot." With her heart torn up over her mom and dealing with her sister, Piper's life was one big mess, like fishing line tangled up in the hook. She couldn't even fantasize about a *'ship*, as Libby would say, with a widowed guy who was dealing with his own drama. She didn't know the first thing about the man's faith or values either, although he'd mentioned Sunday school...and his devotion to his son spoke volumes. She knew as a kid he'd gone to church with his parents, but did he have faith of his own?

And despite what Libby said about Alex eyeing Piper with interest, it wasn't like he'd mentioned seeing her again.

Alex pushed open the door to Java Creek and ushered Jake inside. He stopped abruptly as his gaze zoomed to the backside of the redhead at the end of the line. He'd hardly slept last night for thinking of this woman. And now she stood like a vision before him. One in a straight black skirt, knee-high dark-brown riding boots, a black wool jacket, and a knitted cream headband thingy. The combination added a sheen to her coppery hair.

"Wibby!"

Oh yeah. And her sister stood there too.

Jake ran up to the blonde standing beside Piper, as Libby and her endearing sister whirled at the sound of his voice.

"Piper! Wook! I brought your book to read while Dad works on his 'puter." Jake held up the storybook for Piper to view.

Alex lifted his Jake-free hand and stared at it. Jake *never* just let go of his hand and ran off. *Ever.* Granted, he knew his dad was directly behind him. But still. Alex caught Piper's smiling eyes on him, her hand holding the book while Libby lifted his boy into her arms.

His stomach quivered. How did she manage that with a single glance? Heck, it had started when he'd noticed her, uh, ponytail.

"Daddy, Piper and Wibby wike coffee too!" Jake hugged Libby's neck tightly while Piper, her arm behind Libby, lightly rubbed his back.

"Maybe Piper will sign her book for you, if you ask her nicely," Alex said. "And you might be a bit heavy for Libby, buddy."

"No way!" Libby said, moving Jake sideways out of Alex's reach. "I lift bales of hay and heavy buckets at the ranch every day! Jake doesn't even weigh half as much as a bale of hay."

"She's fine, Daddy," Jake said. "But don't weave." Panic flared in his eyes, but he stayed in Libby's arms.

"You know I won't, buddy," Alex assured softly.

"I know," Jake said. "I want to sit with Wibby. You can sit by Piper."

"How about if we let the girls get a word in edgewise?" Alex winked at Jake, who compressed his lips.

"I guess you get second best, Alex." Piper grinned and swirled her ponytail.

Did he make her nervous? "Yeah, poor me. I have to sit next to a gorgeous woman while I drink my coffee. My life's pretty rough." Her effect on his equilibrium staggered him. He hadn't lurched backward, had he? He scanned his feet. Nope. Planted in the same spot. Whew.

"We're meeting Piper's friend here," Libby said. "She's always late. But sure, you guys can join us." She squeezed Jake closer to her. "Hey, after we have coffee, we're going to church. You guys wanna come with us?" Libby's eyes questioned Alex.

Piper jabbed her sister in the ribs but affirmed her sister's invitation. "It sounds like you're here to work, so ignoring us is fine too."

Ignore Piper? No way. True, he'd meant to get in an hour on the new drone app before Sunday services. But who cared about drones right now?

"The church is just a few blocks from here, and you gentlemen would surely be welcome." Piper reached around Libby again and ruffled Jake's sandy hair.

Barring another business upset, this would be Alex's first service since coming to town. He'd had to silence some client uprisings the last two Sundays.

And look what he'd missed because of it—red hair and a chocolate gaze. Stunning combo.

"Can we go with Wibby and Piper, Daddy?" Jake wriggled in excitement, and Libby set him on the floor.

"Sure, buddy. We were headed there in a bit anyway."

"They have Sunday school for boys your age," Libby said to Jake.

"Can Dad go with me?"

"Piper's friend, Callie, teaches that class. I'm sure she'll let your dad in." The blonde sent a sly look Piper's direction.

"I'm sure Callie will," Piper said, deadpan.

Chapter 5

Despite Piper's protests, Alex had insisted on buying all the drinks. A foursome had just departed some cozy leather seating by a window, so Libby and Jake dashed off to nab the chairs.

Piper ambled toward the seating, with Alex beside her. She parked her toffee mocha and Callie's butterscotch latte on the table in front of Jake and Libby and sat across from the two kids, who had separate club chairs. Alex plopped beside Piper on the love seat. His left arm, encased in black leather, brushed lightly against her as he set his blueberry-flavored coffee and Jake's strawberry frappe on the table.

Piper looked around in a daze. It wasn't cold in the coffee shop. She couldn't blame her lightheadedness on freezing temperatures this time. But how could this guy who didn't even live on her side of the—

"Hey, you guys didn't save me a seat!" Callie called out as she dragged a green-painted high-back chair toward them, her platinum hair swirling around her.

"We were lucky to get this spot," Piper replied. "I was just about to grab a chair and set it here."

"Ahh, you bought my coffee! Thanks!" Callie plunked into her chair and picked up the cup Piper had edged toward her.

"Actually, my friend Alex bought the drinks."

Always a bundle of energy, Callie nearly crackled with electricity this morning. Piper hoped her friend didn't zap anyone.

Callie took a quick sip of her latte. Her eyes drifted closed as she relished the flavor. When they opened again, she glanced between Alex and Jake. "Umm, I don't think we've met. I'm sure we haven't because...I'd have remembered you two."

Callie flashed her vivacious grin at Alex, and Piper groaned inwardly. Her friend had no filter, and Piper couldn't predict what would pop out of her mouth. She made quick introductions.

"Alex and Jake stopped by the ranch yesterday, and we ran into them here just a few minutes ago." With her eyes, Piper implored Callie to restrain her words.

"They're going to church with us. Jake will be in your class, Callie," Libby said.

"My dad too," Jake said.

"Hi, Jake. We'll have lots of fun in my class. Your dad too," Callie said, raising an eyebrow toward Piper and Alex.

Later, Piper mouthed.

"Did you tell Libby yet?" Callie asked Piper, the abrupt change in conversation typical of her.

Oh, their friendship was so over! Callie just couldn't keep her mouth shut about anything. No, Piper hadn't told Libby, and now wasn't the time. Not in front of Jake and Alex.

"Tell me what?" Libby asked, tilting her head as she lowered the cup that had been on its way to her lips.

Piper silently begged Callie to shut her mouth.

"I can't believe she didn't tell you," Callie said. "She was so excited..."

I really need to work on my telepathic powers. With her finger, Piper drew a cutting motion across her throat.

Callie ignored her.

Alex stared at her.

Libby's eyes accused her.

"Piper had this really great idea for Christmas. The women at the church are going to knit or crochet hats, and she's going to invite families with foster children to the ranch to see the new cria—hopefully two crias..."

Oh, why won't you keep quiet for once? Piper pressed the back of her head against the love seat, feeling Alex's curious stare on her and Libby's glower searing her skin. She didn't need to look at Libby to gauge her reaction.

"...and you'll give away the hats to the kids and their foster brothers and sisters. I'm heavily involved with the foster parent program already, and I'm going to help. We're going to get a huge tree for the barn and—"

Libby jumped up. "Not happening. We are not celebrating Christmas. Piper already agreed." She paced behind Callie's chair.

Piper shot to her feet and blazed a look in Callie's direction. "No, I hadn't told Libby, thank you very much. I planned a different approach." She sighed. Another scene in front of Alex. Could life get any more chaotic? He must think she was a terrible sister. Did she care?

She crossed to her sister and placed an arm across her shoulders to halt her pacing. "Baby, we can't just ignore Christmas. We don't have to have our own celebration, but I thought this might be a way for us to...to...maybe try to make it special. It's Christmas..."

"We're not doing this, sis. Not without Mom. We are not celebrating Christmas. You said!" Stomping her ankle-booted feet, Libby swerved around Piper's outstretched hand. "And I'm outta here."

That girl is so unreasonable! Seething, Piper stood her ground. She wouldn't chase after her. It wouldn't do any good. She was so stubborn. There was just no reaching her. Let her wander around in the freezing weather in nothing but a stupid tank top and that ridiculous Mickey Mouse sweatshirt Dad had bought her on their only trip to Disneyland, just before he'd been killed on a domestic disturbance call. Piper had long given up trying to get Libby to wear any kind of church clothes. That was one battle not worth pursuing.

Callie had witnessed multiple explosions from Libby in the last two months, though this was the first one she'd triggered.

But Alex...

Jake had curled himself into his dad's lap when Libby jetted out of her chair. Alex fully expected Jake to bury his face in his chest, but instead he watched Libby and Piper with avid interest.

Alex's heart went out to Piper as Libby stomped her way around tables toward the do—

Jake sprang off Alex's legs. Startled, Alex gawked at his empty lap, his arms still positioned as if around his son, who now chugged after Libby.

Jake never left him behind. He just didn't—except now he'd done it twice in as many days. Alex snapped his mouth shut when Piper flicked him a quick glance before crossing her arms over her chest. The urge to comfort her overpowered him, and he rose, unsteady on his feet as his mind reeled with Jake's defection.

He could certainly get used to this.

"Wibby! Wait! Wibby!"

Alex groaned as his son's childish voice rang out like Christmas bells at a library, alerting other patrons to the scene. Heads turned as Jake's little legs propelled him toward the irate teenager.

While Callie sat with her mouth in an O, Alex sauntered up behind Piper and bracketed her shoulder with his arm just as Libby put her hand on the door. Jake shouted her name once more.

Alex felt Piper gulp in the caffeinated air but not let it out. He found himself holding his breath along with her as Libby paused by the exit framed by clear minibulbs twinkling the promise of the Christmas Libby disdained.

"She'll keep going. Her…despair over Mom's leaving overwhelms her sometimes," Piper muttered.

"And Jake will turn around in a second, spooked that I'm not beside him." Alex gave a gentle squeeze, afraid the action would alert Piper to the fact that he held her, afraid that she wouldn't notice. He smiled inwardly. What a great dilemma. But when she slightly nestled into his loose embrace, he drew her closer, enjoying the moment despite the commotion neither of them needed.

He expected to have to let her go any second now, to soothe his panicked son.

Mesmerized, he watched as Libby stiffened her back and faced the sidewalk, the glimmering bulbs creating almost an aura around her.

"Wibby, I wuv Christmas. My dad says it's Jesus's birthday." Jake stopped just behind her and placed a hand on one of her jean-clad legs.

The air whooshed out of Alex as Libby knelt before his son, scooping him into a tight clinch.

"I'll celebrate with you, Wibby." Jake patted her shoulder with one hand.

Piper looked heavenward. Alex could make out her silent words—*Thank You, Father.*

"Usually she just storms off and wanders around for a couple hours before returning all defiant. Something about Jake reaches out to her in a way...in a way..." She cleared her throat and blinked. "In a way I just don't seem to be able to."

She lifted a grateful gaze to Alex and twisted slightly in his arms.

He looked at the woman who'd filled his thoughts all night. How easy and almost natural it would be to lean down and enjoy their mutual relief even more by capturing the lips smiling up at him. He dipped his head slightly before sanity made its unwelcome return. At the same time, Callie dived toward Piper and pulled her from Alex into her own tight hug.

"I'm so sorry, Piper. Me and my super-big mouth. Gigantic mouth. I'm such a dope." She released Piper and slanted a look from Alex to Jake, who tugged a resistant Libby back toward their group.

To Alex's relief, the other customers returned to their java and pastries, and the coffeehouse buzzed with low conversation again.

Callie tipped her head to one shoulder and then the other. "Who exactly *are* you two guys?"

Mortified by the morning's events, Piper had planned to sit as far away from Alex at church as possible, but that was thwarted by Jake lurching down the carpeted aisle after

Sunday school, holding his dad's hand but two steps ahead of him. Did that boy ever just walk?

The elegant Mrs. Saunders followed several steps behind in their father-son wake. At least she hadn't been present to witness Piper and Libby's verbal tussle. Or Alex's almost kiss. Had she dreamed that? Probably, but she could still vividly picture his lips heading toward hers.

An audible groan slipped between her lips. She didn't know the Saunderses well. And Mrs. Saunders surely knew of Piper and Libby's saga. What had she said to Alex? It couldn't have been anything good. Libby always in trouble. Piper incapable of handling her wayward sister. She glanced around for an escape, for anyone who might need her attention.

"My grandma says you and Wibby can sit by us," Jake announced as he reached up to capture her hand while still holding Alex's with the other.

His sweet innocence compelled her to meet him on his level, and she crouched.

"Hey, buddy, Piper and Libby can sit wherever they please."

Alex bent and palmed her shoulder with his hand. His slightly raspy voice wrapped itself around her like an embrace. "Hi again, Piper," he added softly.

Piper scanned his hazel eyes flickering with indecision. Was he as uncomfortable as she was? Jake certainly wasn't.

"I know, Daddy," he said, letting go of his father and perching himself on Piper's knee as his dad straightened. He swung an arm around her neck. "But they want to sit by us, don't you, Piper?"

No with a capital N. "Sure, Jake. Libby and I would love to sit by you." She slid him off her knee, stood, and placed her hand on a nearby solid-oak pew. Light streaming through long stained-glass windows created rainbow markings on its back—the best kind of special effects during a worship service.

These old pews had been supporting the congregation since the mid-nineteen hundreds. Church members had talked periodically of replacing them with chairs, but that always caused such a stir with the seniors that the subject never gained traction. Piper was kind of glad. She leaned against the pew for support and slowly realized Jake was still talking.

"...and my dad and papa and grandma," Jake added, clearly for Piper's benefit.

"Oh, of...course." Piper knew she shouldn't be so concerned about what Mrs. Saunders might have mentioned to Alex, but she cringed at the imagined dialogue between mother and son.

She gave herself a mental shake. It really didn't matter. It wasn't as if she and Alex were dating. They hadn't even had a single conversation without spectators. The near kiss had been in a crowded coffee shop, in front of Callie and Libby and Jake and who knew how many others! And having, no less, connected with him only yesterday. If she ever did kiss this guy—her pulse stepped up its pace at the mere thought—she didn't want kids or gawkers.

But the likelihood they'd get to know each other well enough for that was downright low, with her taking care of a sister who argued at every turn, not to mention that Alex's son was glued to his side. And why would he want to get to know her anyway, after witnessing not one but two flare-ups between her and Libby in under twenty-four hours?

If she were really trying to attract a guy—which she wasn't, of course!—she'd have to change her strategy. Or lock her sister in her room when he was around. As appealing as that might be...

"Hi, Piper." Mrs. Saunders offered a genuine, warm smile when she reached the trio. The eyes under her winged brows were equally as cordial. In her blue wool pencil skirt with matching blazer, black velvet ankle boots, and her short light-brown A-frame-styled hair the same color as Alex's, she certainly didn't look old enough to be the mother of anyone Alex's age. If Piper remembered correctly, he was at least three years older than her twenty-three.

Mrs. Saunders's cheery greeting made Piper doubt her previous negative thoughts toward the woman.

"Good morning, Mrs. Saunders," she responded.

Alex's mom pulled her close for a brief hug. She'd never hugged Piper before! Their relationship had apparently moved to a new level.

"Isobel, dear. Isobel. I'm sure I've asked you to call me that before. And my husband is Grant, not Mr. Saunders. Ever since Jake met Libby yesterday, it's been nothing but 'Wibby' at my—"

"Grandma, not 'Wibby.' I said 'Wibby!'"

"Oh, Jake," his contrite grandmother said, "of course. I meant Libby. I meant *Libby.* It's been nothing but 'Libby' at our house." She hugged the boy to her side.

"Have you visited your parents before?" Piper asked Alex. "Did I miss you? I only made it over once in a while when I lived in Spokane."

"This is the first time I've been to Cranberry Creek since my parents moved here permanently, since...since Amy..." He left the rest unsaid as his Adam's apple bobbed. "I probably could have just asked Mom or Dad where you lived rather than looking your ranch up on Google. I never even thought—"

"There's Wibby!"

Once back at his parents' house after the church service, Alex helped Jake change into a clean Tranformers T-shirt, this one with Grimlock on the front, and hustled him out the door. He'd take Jake for a walk near the creek. Anything to avoid his mom. He could tell she was about to add a hundred questions to the ones he'd answered yesterday about his visit to Criations. She'd mentioned that Piper and Libby might be at church, but he hadn't anticipated running into them at the downtown coffee shop. And nearly kissing Piper… He was quickly developing a *thing* for this particular redhead. And for chocolate eyes. And freckles.

He tingled at the memory and had to check to make sure the current hadn't transferred to Jake's hand. Since his son didn't jerk away, Alex figured only he'd experienced the voltage.

The trail behind his parents' home led past their small Gala apple orchard and directly to a path that ran parallel to Cranberry Creek. Jake had reminded Alex he'd promised to take him to the creek soon, and today made the perfect day. Mom and Dad would be busy making lunch for another hour at least.

And despite the chilly weather, the sunshine had tempted him beyond what he could endure. Such a relief following day after day after day of gray, cloudy skies and constant drizzle in Seattle. He lifted his face to the blinding rays. Good thing Mom had reminded him to grab his sunglasses before he'd left. As much as he loved salty air and his Space Needle view, he could get used to this.

Alex angled a finger to his right, toward the snow-mantled mountain appearing in a dip between the beautiful but desolate sagebrush hills surrounding the property. "See that mountain, Jake?"

"Yeah! I know! Mount Rainier. You said that!"

"Not exactly," Alex muttered. "See, Mount Rainier is what we see when we're in Seattle." As the pathway narrowed, he dropped Jake's hand and let his son walk ahead of him a few steps.

"I saw it on the plane too, when we flew home!"

Alex hadn't thought this would be so tricky. He and Jake had traveled to Seattle on the previous two Fridays for staff meetings and had flown right back the next afternoon. The tip of Mount Rainier had risen through tenacious clouds both times, a true icon in the sky.

"Yes, but that's not this mountain. This is a different one. Mount Adams."

"Is it higher than Rainier?"

"Nope. Remember I told you Rainier was the highest in Washington?"

"But is Mount Adams taller?"

"No, highest means tallest."

Jake stopped, and Alex tripped over him, tumbling to the ground and taking Jake with him.

"Sorry, buddy! I wasn't expecting you to stop," Alex said as he rolled onto his side. He placed his elbow under himself and propped his head in his palm. "Are you okay?"

"I'm fine, Daddy." Jake sat up. "Why aren't we getting up?"

"Why'd you stop, Jake?" Alex asked, letting himself fall back on the ground, his knees up, his eyes on his son.

"I saw that mountain before! When we were at Wibby's! I remember!"

"Yeah, they have a pretty darn good view of it, don't they."

Jake pushed up and brushed off his knees. "Get up, Daddy. I wanna see the creek. And I wanna go back to Wibby's."

"You just saw her today! Twice."

"So?"

So indeed. Alex's sentiments exactly. Only about Piper.

Chapter 6

Piper lit the gas log in the great room and flopped onto the shag rug in front of the fireplace. She really wanted to sit in front of the woodstove in the family room, but anytime it was cold enough to burn wood, the county declared a burn ban for air quality. So a gas fire it was.

She leaned against the indigo down-blend sofa and propped her knitting bag beside her on the right. She opened her knitting needle booklet—one she'd designed herself to hold her circular and double-pointed knitting needles—and pulled out a size 8 sixteen-inch circular. She grabbed a strand of silver-gray undyed chunky alpaca-wool blend yarn, spun from her alpacas, from the ceramic yarn bowl on her left and cast on sixty-eight stitches, the correct number for a middle-grade child's hat. The clack of her white-brass-plated needles, handling the cushy-soft alpaca yarn, soothed her frayed nerves. She and Libby had been arguing two days straight about Piper's Christmas idea. Libby continued to insist they skip Christmas altogether like they were doing for Thanksgiving on Thursday, while Piper insisted they celebrate by doing something special for less fortunate children.

After seeing Jake's reaction to the alpacas on Saturday, Piper had dashed off to Callie's downtown yarn store,

Imagknitive, and while Piper knit up a hat pattern she'd been designing, she and Callie brainstormed about a way to involve foster kids with Piper's animals. It couldn't be anything grand scale, as Piper and Libby ran the ranch by themselves, though Callie helped occasionally, as did a few homeschooled kids, for science credits.

Callie, who occasionally parented a foster child and had connections to the Children's Administration, had suggested hosting an event for foster families, as there were only a few in the Cranberry Creek area.

Piper had intended to bribe Libby into accepting the plan with a couple of Ding Dongs and returned ownership of her phone. They needed to do something special for Christmas! But she should have known Callie would blab.

Now on top of the arguing, Piper hadn't seen or heard from Alex since Sunday, and she missed him. Which was ridiculous, since she barely knew the guy. It wasn't like he had her phone number anyway. And she wasn't in the church directory his mom probably had, as she'd moved away for college five years ago. But he knew where she lived!

After eight rounds of knit 1, purl 1, she laid her project flat to measure the ribbing—about two inches. Great! She hated doing the ribbing, and now she could start the pattern stitch. But when she glanced closer, she groaned. She hadn't made sure the stitches weren't twisted on the needle before she'd begun knitting, and now the whole ribbing kinked out of shape. A rookie mistake! She knew better when it came to circs. She flipped the needle from the stitches and started frogging the project, curly wool heaping back into her yarn bowl. She couldn't concentrate for all the arguing and missing Alex and Jake. So much for knitting therapy.

And then the back door slammed.

Yay. Libby was home from school. Piper pulled her knees up, placed her elbows on them, and buried her head in her arms.

"Hey, Piper, I know you're here. I saw your Jeep. No more school until Monday!"

Libby tromped into the great room and plopped onto the sofa.

Piper propped one arm up on the empty cushion behind her and tipped her chin to gaze at her sister, tensing her shoulders at the arguing that would commence any second now.

"Oh, and you should know. Alex and Jake are on their way over. They're coming for dinner." She shifted her backpack off her shoulders and placed it next to her on the sofa. At Piper's glare, she dropped it to the floor with a thud.

Piper scrambled to her feet, knocking her yarn bowl over and scattering the alpaca fiber onto the shag area rug and hardwood floor.

"How do you know they're coming over?" She glanced down at her jeans and green cable-knit sweater—a project from two years ago—relieved she looked presentable. She flicked her ponytail holder off her wrist and fussed her curls into a ponytail.

"Whoa, sis, you must have it bad for this guy. Getting all dolled up." Libby cocked her head and lifted one corner of her lips. "I know I'm crazy about Jake. That kid's just the cutest in the whole world. And that dad of his—"

"I don't have it bad for Alex. I have it bad for Jake." Piper huffed. "And putting my hair into a ponytail is hardly dolled up. Wait. Why are they coming for dinner? How did this happen? And did you think you were cooking?" *Ha! Not a chance.* Piper had already started dinner, and Libby was a terrible cook. Though she did bake the best oatmeal scotchie cookies ever.

Piper knelt to scoop her now tangled yarn back into its bowl. She'd deal with it later.

"Of course not! They probably want something other than mac and cheese or ramen. I ran to Java Creek for a mocha at lunch, and Alex was there with Jake, working on an app. He designs apps. Isn't that cool? I asked him for one to make pesky sisters disappear."

"Yeah, pesky little sisters!" Piper grinned.

"Anyway, Jake was playing with a Transformer and looking at your book! He loves that story. I read it to him before heading back to class."

Piper paused with a handful of yarn dangling from her fingers and turned to look at Libby. Her voice sounded like she was...smiling. Indeed, she beamed one of her rare, genuine smiles, showing off her gleaming white teeth.

For a moment, Piper basked in it. It wouldn't last, and who knew when she'd see it directed her way again.

"Jake asked if they could come see Sophia. I told him dinner's at six and to be here by four."

By four! That was only an hour away!

"Hurry and go change, Libby. We need to make sure there's warm water in all the bowls. It's supposed to drop below freezing tonight. And I was hoping we could get that plywood nailed to the rest of the shelters to keep the wind out. We should have finished winterizing them weeks ago." Maybe that one could wait until tomorrow.

"I told Jake he could help me water, ride with me on the ATV. Maybe I'll take him out to the pasture," Libby said, as though Jake rode with her every day.

Piper dropped the yarn end into the bowl, stood up, and tugged her sweater down more solidly around her hips. "That won't work. I told you about Jake. I don't know why exactly, but since his mom died, he won't leave his dad's side."

"Yeah, well, we'll see about that. You just worry about dinner. I'll take care of the animals tonight. And Jake. We'll figure something out."

Huh? Piper cast a suspicious glance at her sister. She *never* volunteered to take care of anything by herself.

Libby picked up Piper's knitting needle booklet, opened the vinyl flap holding a circ, and pulled the needle out. "Whatcha makin'?"

Piper bent to retrieve the yarn bowl and scooted it underneath the end table. She sat back on her haunches, her eyes on the fire. Anywhere but on Libby. "I'm making a kid's hat. For our Christmas event. Which I'm calling Christmas at Criations: Kids and Crias. And if Sophia's twins live, sharing that with the children would be so special, even if it's only for a few hours. Dominique and Fresca are especially good with kids, and Sophia loves attention. It's happening, Libby. It's gonna be good. And you're going to be part of it."

She turned her head, clenching her teeth when Libby's eyes flashed daggers at her. Here it came. The arguing. They'd probably be screaming at each other when Alex and Jake showed up.

But then Libby's blue eyes drooped slightly, and her lashes dipped, shading them. She lifted the circular needle she held in front of her. "I'd better get started on mine too," she muttered. "For Jake. He said he 'wuved' my hat today. When I told him you knitted it for me, he asked if I could make one for him. He said he's been praying for snow." She picked up Piper's knitting bag and pulled out several hanks of double-knitting-weight yarns. "He's got those gorgeous hazel eyes. I'm thinking this nubby brown alpaca blend would be perfect for him."

What, no argument? No shouting match? No stomping out and skipping chores again? Piper nearly tumbled backward on her heels. After two days of quarreling, Libby had been won over by a scrappy preschooler? She hadn't mentioned the Christmas event, but knowing her sister, Piper understood this was her way of saying that maybe she'd cooperate, without actually saying she would. And Piper wouldn't press her luck.

At least, not right now. Libby hadn't picked up a set of knitting needles since Dad died. She'd knitted him a dozen hats over the years, which he'd worn proudly. Piper felt as if some small miracle had taken place somewhere today.

As Libby measured out yarn to cast on to her circs, Piper dashed to the kitchen, saying, "Lucky for you, I put an elk roast on the Traeger late this morning. I need to get the potatoes on pronto though." She'd intended the roast to provide a couple days of leftovers for the two of them, but she'd figure out the rest of the week later. Neither one of them enjoyed cooking much. Mom had been the one who loved to spend hours in the kitchen.

Piper skidded to a stop in front of the kitchen pantry. Did Jake and Alex eat game? Her father had been a hunter, and they still had some elk, venison, duck pepperoni, and quail in the deep freezer. She and Libby had grown up on wild game. But would Alex and Jake even eat it?

They lived in Seattle. Maybe they were vegetarians. Piper cringed.

Well, she didn't have time to make anything else.

She scrubbed and cut the red potatoes into quarters and then sliced carrots into the mix. She placed them into a cast-iron oblong dish, added a tablespoon of coconut oil, and sprinkled on some seasoning. She opened the sliding glass door from the dining room to the back deck and stepped out to place the dish on the smoker/barbecue, next to the roast.

She hadn't known how to turn it on when she'd moved home two months ago. YouTube had fixed that, and now it was almost all she used.

It was near freezing, and she only had her chunky-knit sweater on, but she stood on the deck with her heart welling in gratitude.

Father, please help me not to provoke my sister tonight. And help her, Father, to somehow, someway, find the joy of Jesus this Christmas. Use me to comfort her. I will give You all the glory.

She hadn't spent enough time giving Him glory since Mom left. She swallowed hard at her neglect. It had been difficult to find the good in it. But she and Libby had each other. They were healthy. Mom had left plenty of money in the ranch account to pay Criations' bills, and several of their crias would command top prices, so at least the farm and most of their living expenses were covered. Illustrating paid the rest.

And they had company coming!

She didn't know why, but she felt a little like jumping up and down and clapping her hands. Jake and Alex would be here before dinner!

The tingles just wouldn't stop.

Alex pulled his pickup into Piper's driveway and parked next to her Jeep. He swiped his clammy palms down his jeans just as Jake's feet punched his seat.

"Jake, I told you to stop doing that."

"I did it, Dad. I unbuckled myself. Can I get out? The door's wocked."

Alex could hear Jake flipping the handle up and down. He had drilled Jake about not ever opening the car door himself. So much for that.

"If you'd asked first instead of grabbing the handle, I might have let you. But now you have to wait for me to open the door."

"Hurry, Dad. Wibby and Sophia are waiting for me."

Alex grinned as he slid off his seat and opened his son's door. Jake's almost-four-year-old self was pretty well centered on...himself.

"Well, we can't have that, buddy."

Jake hopped out of his seat and walked straight to the blond teen, who waited at the tire swing.

Alex scanned the yard and paddocks but didn't spot Piper. He wondered what would happen if he didn't stay behind Jake, if he wandered to the front door. Jake could still see him. Dare he risk it?

Too late. Libby had already gathered Jake into her arms, and Alex's son was waving to him.

"C'mon, Daddy. Wibby's over here."

Alex sniffed the air. What was that delicious smoky aroma? He hoped he and Jake weren't putting the redhead out too much, but honestly, he wouldn't have cared if she'd served Frosted Flakes, just for another glance at her, to hear her sweet soprano voice some more. Heck, he could have picked up some Chinese on the way. Why hadn't he thought of that earlier? He hung his head.

They were here on a whim. He hoped Piper wasn't mad.

But maybe if she was, he could smooth her ruffled feathers with a grin. Not that that had ever worked on a woman before, but maybe she'd be the first. Okay, he'd never seriously dated anyone other than Amy. Not that he was dating Piper.

Oh! Just thinking about her turned him into a bundle of nerves.

But he did have a plan to charm Piper into forgiving him for this impromptu visit if he needed it. He knew he shouldn't have relied on Libby's invitation alone, but he'd wanted to come so badly, he'd neglected to ask for Piper's phone number.

So here he stood, wishing he could bundle Piper into his arms. And he hadn't even seen her yet.

"Dad, come over here," Jake said as he squirmed out of the swing.

Alex strode up to the teenager now holding his boy's mitten-covered hand in hers. "Hi, Libby. Thanks for the invitation. Are you sure Piper doesn't mind? Is she around? We should go say hi to her too, Jake."

"Where is she, Wibby? Where's Piper? Can she come out and play too?" Jake tugged on Libby's hand.

Alex heard a door click shut behind him and swiveled to see Piper jogging toward the fence. Before she reached them, Libby lowered herself in front of Jake, completely on her knees before him. Alex found the gesture humbling and sensitive. She really cared about his son. She lifted her blue gaze toward Alex and Piper, who'd stopped nearby but hadn't spoken yet.

He chanced a sideways look at Piper, who said hi to him and Jake. The wonder of sunlight glinting off her copper hair replaced the oxygen in Alex's lungs, as if he'd jumped a dozen hurdles at full speed, with Jake on his back. If he reached out to take Piper's hand, would she put it in his?

He kept his hand at his side. What if she didn't take it? Why was he so afraid? He focused on exhaling the wonder from his lungs and inhaling the pure, chilled valley air.

"Jake..." Libby hesitated.

What was the teenager up to?

"I have to refill the water in the paddocks and check a fence post in the pasture. I'm going to ride that four-wheel ATV over there." She pointed to the small carport at the side of the house. "I...I thought you could go with me. Do you want to ride with me?"

Alex's breath hitched. Would he ever actually breathe again around these women?

"I...I... Can Daddy ride it too?" Jake shrank toward Alex but still hung on to Libby's hand.

Libby stayed on her knees and pulled Jake into a loose hug. "No, it's only big enough for me and you, and only because you're a kid yet."

"But what if my dad gets scared when I'm out there?"

Alex choked down the thorn that had settled in his throat. He knelt to one knee before Libby and Jake, and Piper did the same.

He skimmed his gaze over the blonde and his son and finally Piper. The warmth of this woman and her sister, fraught with their own hardships, enveloped him, and surely his son too.

"I'll only be a little scared, Jake. I'll stay outside so I can see you."

Libby spun on her knees, pulling Jake with her. She pointed to a dog lolling against a side fence. "See that big white dog, Jake? That's Brisco. He's a Great Pyrenees, super friendly, and he loves kids and dads. He guards the alpacas and keeps little critters out of our pastures. We have three of them out there—Brisco, Sadie, and Dulce. How about if we call Brisco over here to guard your dad while we're in the pasture? C'mere, Brisco!" She patted her hands, covered with canvas work gloves, on her legs.

The dog scrambled to his feet and trotted toward Libby. She opened the display gate, ran down the laneway, slid open another gate, and led him to Jake.

"Go ahead and pet Brisco," Libby directed. "He loves kids, and he won't bite. You can love on him all you want."

Jake needed no more encouragement as he flung his arms around Brisco's neck. The canine flipped his head up and down, rubbing against Jake.

Alex raised an eyebrow at Piper.

She laughed. "I should have thought of that sooner. These dogs are guardians in a real sense. They're attuned to people too, and they know when a person, especially a kid, could use an extra dose of doggie love."

"But Jake is all over him," Alex said as his son buried his face in the dog's fur. "Should I pull him off?"

"No, he's not pulling his tail or ears or tugging his fur out," Piper said, her hand on Alex's elbow. "They'll be fine."

"Can I take him home?" Jake asked as the large dog flopped to the ground. Jake followed suit, securing an arm around Brisco's back.

"He has to stay here and take care of Sophia," Libby said before Alex could say no. "And if you're going to help me with the Christmas event here, like we talked about at the coffee shop"—she cast a quick, guilty glance at Piper, who blinked as if in shock—"you'll need to know how to ride on an ATV with me. And how to take care of the alpacas."

"Did you hear that, Daddy?" Jake lifted his palms to his

sides. "I get to help Wibby with the Christmas party! We might have to come here every day prob'ly. You stay outside, Daddy. I'm going to ride the A...A...what's it called?"

"ATV," Libby inserted.

"ATV. Stay outside. And keep Brisco by you, Daddy."

"I will. And I'll wave to you when you're out there. And you keep an eye on Libby!"

The teen chuckled. "Your dad thinks I need a babysitter, Jake."

She clasped his hand. "If you're going to help me on the ranch," she said as they headed toward the carport, "we're going to need to get you some real work boots."

"Wike yours? With that wittle flap?"

"Just like mine, with that little flap. And hey, we'll stop and see Sophia before heading to the pasture."

Jake trotted beside Libby and looked back at Alex only once.

Alex grinned at Piper. He might not exactly be alone with her, but this was probably as close as he would get to that in the foreseeable future. And not only was Jake not beside him, but Piper and her sister weren't at each other's throats.

A victory, for sure.

Chapter 7

Oh, that girl! Acting huffy with Piper, when she'd been discussing Christmas plans with a three-year-old boy! But as Piper glanced from Alex's wide-eyed expression to Libby showing Jake the ATV, she couldn't help but marvel at her sister too. A total rebel one minute, a little boy's best friend the next.

Not wanting to disturb Alex's trancelike state, Piper stayed still as a fence post, gazing the same direction as the man still too stunned to talk. Jake helped Libby heft the five-gallon water buckets that Piper had filled earlier onto the ATV, and they headed toward the laneway.

Piper stuffed her hands into her jacket pockets. She should have grabbed a pair of gloves before racing outside, but her rush to see Alex had pushed rational thoughts aside. She allowed herself to peruse the man. Leather jacket in this freezing weather, no hat or gloves, but a trendy knit scarf around his neck. Light-brown hair arranged in a kind of Seattle-preppy swept-up-above-his-forehead style, a five o'clock shadow gracing his jawline.

A vision popped into Piper's head. She saw herself placing a scarf she'd knit around his neck. As if that would ever happen. Even so, her mind filtered through various yarn possibilities, through what would go with his hair, his eyes. Fiber from one of her alpacas. Samson's ginger wool might be perfect. Maybe a reverse stockinette stitch or seed stitch or a simple slip stitch...

Piper's chest squeezed tight, an unfamiliar sensation that had her drawing in deep gulps of air. And her stomach. Surely that was just a hunger pang. Hunger for the man in front of her?

She blew out her breath. He was so much easier to think about than dealing with Libby. But how long before she set Piper off again, or Piper sent her sister into a tirade? Why had Libby invited them to dinner, and how could Piper keep it from turning into a disaster?

Alex turned toward her and reached out a hand, his long, strong fingers mesmerizing her. He would be so easy to lean on, to absorb some of her heartache, but she couldn't do that. His eyes still reflected his own sadness, something mysterious. Sure, he was a widower, but there was something more. And whatever was going on with Jake had to be fairly serious.

Nonetheless, she put her hand in his, and the warmth of his fingers spread heat not just to her hand but to her core.

And when he smiled, well, a woman's heart rate really did speed up when the right guy flashed his pearly whites at her.

"I can't believe he went with her," Alex said. "Jake has what's called separation anxiety disorder. At first I didn't know what was happening after Amy...passed away, and I didn't get help soon enough. I took him to a pediatrician a few months ago, but he said Jake would outgrow it, which isn't happening. And it's so severe now, I just haven't known what to do."

"He's such a sweet boy," Piper said. "Even with that, you've done a good job with him."

Alex rubbed the pad of his thumb over the top of her hand, almost absentmindedly, as if he did that all the time. "Amy and my marriage..." He looked as if he wanted to say more, his expression somber. He sighed. "I'll just say it was...pretty difficult sometimes. And then I came here, thanks to my mom insisting we celebrate the holidays with them. And we met the two of you." His Adam's apple dipped, and he squeezed her hand. "Occasionally I spend a half hour or so without him after he goes to bed, but I'm usually so exhausted myself, I fall asleep when he does. He starts his days pretty darn early."

Piper held her breath, afraid if she let it out, he'd stop talking or let go of her hand. But she managed to squeak out, "And now he's off with Libby for a bit, and you're stuck here with me."

She smiled when he threw his head back and laughed, deep and hearty.

She definitely needed to rein in her thoughts. Between their two families, an emotional calamity seemed more likely than a romantic prospect. And she might break under the weight of any more drama. But right now, she rather enjoyed the shift to a lighter vibe.

"Alone, or practically alone anyway, with a beautiful redhead. I'd give up *me* time for that any day! And a redhead who's cooking me dinner to boot. What was that delicious smell? I noticed it first thing when we pulled in." He crinkled his nose.

Piper hesitated. Did she tell him? "I put a...roast on my dad's smoker-slash-grill earlier today." She released his hand to take her phone out of her pocket and swiped to the Traeger app to check the meat's temperature. "You got lucky. I'm not a great cook. But Dad bought this fancy grill before he died."

Alex squeezed her arm gently, and the sympathetic gesture spread bubbles of emotion through her.

"He called it his new 'grillfriend.'"

Alex chuckled and rubbed his hand up and down her arm.

"When I moved back home from Spokane, I was determined to figure it out. I didn't want it to just sit there and go to waste."

"I feel like we kind of thrust ourselves on you tonight." He twisted to survey Libby and Jake, who had stopped to fill the water bowl in the young males paddock. "She's the one who keeps inviting us here."

Piper grinned. "I never know what Libby will do! We always seem to get into it when the two of you are around. And I can't even guarantee that tonight will be any better." *That girl better behave herself for one night, one dinner!* She could count their company on one hand—Callie and sometimes Emi, the ranch's veterinarian and Piper's childhood friend. Maybe a couple of Libby's friends, but they always holed themselves up in her room with chips and salsa...and Ding Dongs.

A gust of wind ruffled Piper's ponytail and reminded her about the plywood she really needed to nail around the shelters. If the temperature dropped any lower or the snow came, some of the older females would need coats as well.

"Hey, you haven't seen Sophia yet," Piper said. "You want to meet her? We're expecting her to deliver next month."

"I know. Jake goes on and on about her and her twin crias. Why are they called that?"

"It's Spanish for *baby*." Piper frowned. "If Sophia is in the maternity shelter, you'll be blocked from Jake's view for a bit though."

Alex grimaced and gazed out to the pasture and paddocks again. "I don't know then. You haven't seen him flip out. It can be loud and scary. And his distress is real."

Libby and Jake had nearly reached the water bowl in the young families area.

"But I should see the animal Jake's so entranced with."

She held out her hand, and when he fastened his to it, she wound him through the laneway to the maternity paddock, Brisco trotting at his other side. In the shelter, the dog curled up on the straw and rested his nose on his paws, his eyes on the newcomer, Alex. He looked so cute, like he understood his role in protecting Jake's dad.

He probably did.

Sophia and several other mommies-to-be—though they'd deliver next year—munched on some hay as Piper approached. She pulled a little baggie of grain out of her coat pocket and poured some into her palm and Alex's. "How are you today, baby?" Piper crooned to Sophia. "You're such a good girl. We can't wait for your babies to be born. You'll be a great mommy to twins."

Alex shifted his palm toward Sophia.

"She's had one other cria," Piper said, "and at the same time nurtured another cria when its mother died. Twins won't be a completely new concept to Sophia."

She pulled some straw off the alpaca's belly. "She's an odd duck about being petted. She likes it, but we don't do it often, because they might not respect the natural boundaries between people and alpacas. But you can pet her. Just don't let Jake see. And avoid her head. She's not fond of having her top knot ruffled."

Alex's fingers ambled down the white alpaca's withers.

"Sophia's the one thing that seems to unite me and Libby right now," Piper said as she drew her hand alongside Alex's. "My dad favored spring and fall births, but my mom always wanted a Christmas cria. And now she'll miss the first Christmastime birth on the ranch. This pregnancy was an oops—a gate was left open."

She and Libby lavished attention on Sophia. Special grain treats. A coat on below-freezing nights. Not that the additional care would likely make a difference, but it made them feel like they were helping to ensure survival.

"She's beautiful," Alex said. "And so shaggy. Is that because it's winter?"

Alex's hand followed Piper's now as she continued to stroke Sophia, whose sweet face looked at them with cheerful eyes. "Yes. Our alpacas are huacaya, with the crimpy fleece. Their winter coat helps keep them warm. If it drops into the teens though, I'll have to move her into the barn. But overall, they're rugged creatures and enjoy being outdoors.

"I won't say this in front of Jake, but it's super rare that both twins survive. We've never had twins on the ranch, and we don't know anyone in our region who has. But this year, with Mom being gone, it's just something Libby and I are clinging to, as if it'll make a difference somehow." She ran her hand along Sophia's belly. "It won't be much longer. She's already almost eleven months along."

"Eleven months! How long are they pregnant, anyway?"

Piper chuckled. "About eleven and half months. And should those twins survive, I wanted the kids who come out to the ranch for the Christmas event to be part of something that special. It would be amazing!" She tipped her face up toward Alex, knowing her eyes must be beaming.

When Alex drew her toward him, his other hand still on the alpaca but now covering Piper's too, she laid her forehead against his shoulder, her pulse roaring in her ears, no air in her lungs. She should pull back. She shouldn't grow attached to him. He didn't even live on the east side of the state! And she couldn't leave the ranch or her sister. And then there were her battles with Libby and his struggles with Jake. No way could they be together. But his hand over hers as it rested on the crimpy alpaca fleece, his other arm tightening around her, filtered those arguments out of her mind.

Did his pulse pound with the same intensity as hers? She tipped her head up. He closed his eyes, and the look on his face, as if relishing this unexpected moment, struck a chord in her heart. A joyful chord, a melody she'd never heard, hadn't known existed.

His eyes opened, and he looked directly into hers, the haunted look replaced by a glow of affection.

Her fingers scrunched the leather of one arm of his jacket while her other hand curled around the scarf against his chest. The contrasting textures only heightened her anticipation.

His head dipped. Piper closed her eyes.

"Where's my dad? I don't see my dad. Dad! Dad!"

Wrenching sobs forced Alex to drop his arms from Piper and sent him racing into the paddock. Piper's feet pounded behind him. Jake's cries made him easy to spot, and Alex dashed toward his frantic son, who tugged mercilessly on Libby's hand.

"My dad, my dad. I have to find my dad!" Jake sank to his knees on the ground. "Daddy! Daddy!"

"I'm here, Jake. Right here. I'm coming." Alex slid open the gate to the paddock where Libby hunkered down by his son, rubbing his back. As Alex neared, he could hear her soothing words.

"Your dad's coming, Jake. Look. He's right there. He was in Sophia's paddock. You know where that is, right? He really did stay outside. And hey, look! Brisco's right behind him. I told you he'd guard your dad."

"I'm right here, buddy. I'm right here. Brisco and Piper took good care of me." Alex swept the hiccupping Jake into a tight embrace. "I hadn't seen Sophia yet, and Piper took Brisco along. It's okay. I'm here. I'm here."

Jake wrapped his arms tight around Alex's neck. "When I could...couldn't...f-find you...I...I thought something bad happened, Daddy." He sniffed, and one small hand patted Alex's bicep.

Alex hugged his boy tighter. How could he have been so distracted that he'd forgotten completely about Jake? He knew better! Jake came first. Always. Those few moments before nearly kissing Piper...he hadn't even given a single thought to Jake. How was that possible? It could never happen again.

Yet with his next breath, he wanted it to happen again. He would get therapy for him and Jake, and soon. He might not have known Piper long, but he knew a quality woman when he met one. A girl who rushed home to dedicate herself to caring for her sister and the family ranch was undoubtedly a woman of character. The thought of letting her slip through his fingers scared him more than Jake's panic. As young as Piper was, she'd obviously made sacrifices that had changed the course of her life. Even as Jake's little body shuddered against Alex's chest, he realized how little he knew about her. What *had* she given up? But what he did know impressed the heck out of him, more than any woman he'd ever met.

"You're really okay, Daddy?" Jake pushed himself back from Alex's chest and searched his father's face. "Brisco guarded you?"

Piper walked up alongside Jake and placed a hand on his upper back. "You and your dad are safe on our ranch. Look around." She pointed west. "You see that mountain?"

Jake twisted slightly in Alex's arms. "I do! That's Adams." Jake smiled as another tear rolled down his face. "My daddy told me. He knows everything. He said it's not as high as Rainier."

Piper grinned. "Everything, huh? He's a pretty special guy, that's for sure."

She scrunched her nose at Alex, her grin indicating she'd use that information against him in the future. Oh, she'd have fun with that all right. Alex moaned internally. Even when he held on to a distressed Jake, comforting him, she so easily turned Alex's thoughts away from his son.

It wasn't altogether horrible.

"Do you think he knows that Adams is the second-highest mountain in Washington?"

Jake's head bobbed up and down.

Alex stifled his own grin.

She swung her arm to the north and moved it slowly in a semicircle. "And see those brown hills? In a couple of weeks, they'll be covered with snow. Do you see how protected we are here? And look at all those fences. And the Great Pyrenees dogs. Do you think we'd let anything happen to your dad? The mountains, the hills, the fences, the dogs, they help keep us safe. And don't forget about God. He's watching over you and your dad, over me and Libby too, all the time. You know what the Bible says?"

"Jesus wuvs me?"

Piper's arms spread around Jake and Alex, and even Libby huddled into the circle.

"Yes, that Jesus loves you. But it also says God helps us when we're in trouble."

"God is always wooking down. He never wooks up!" Jake quipped with barely a sniffle.

"Jake, you're so smart!" Libby said. "God *is* always looking down! We're all here for you too, babe. And your dad." She extended her arms.

Alex knew the teenager meant well, but Jake would cling to his dad for hours. He wouldn't be able to set Jake down until bedtime. Getting him into his car seat for the drive to Mom and Dad's would be a mega chore that would lead to more sobbing. But he needed to get his son back to the familiar environment of his grandparents' home pronto.

"Wet me go, Dad." Jake pushed himself away from Alex, leaned toward Libby, and launched himself into her waiting arms.

Once again, Alex didn't know what to do with his empty hands. He looked at Piper, at his hands, at Libby holding his son, whose tears had completely dried up, though they'd left dirty smudges down his cheeks. He'd better hustle Jake into his car seat before he panicked again.

"Come on, buddy. Let's head back to Papa and Grandm—"

"But, Daddy, we didn't even eat yet." Jake snuggled into Libby's shoulder, and she swayed back and forth.

"Yeah, Daddy," she said dryly.

"Yeah, Daddy," Piper added.

They were ganging up on him?

"Besides, we didn't say about spons'ring. You said to keep it a secret. Can we say it now?"

Alex glanced from Piper to Libby, letting his question show in his eyes. If they stayed, Jake might explode again. Were Piper and her sister willing to risk it? Their expressions showed no reservation, and he prayed the evening wouldn't end in a total disaster.

The bratty side of Libby might make an appearance, but Jake seemed to have the same calming effect on her as she had on him. And for some reason, Libby's outbursts didn't derail Jake.

Or Alex.

He stretched his hand to his boy. "Come on, buddy. We'll tell them while we're walking back to the house." He had no idea how Libby would take his idea. He'd meant to mention it to Piper earlier, but her curly red hair and impish smile and the, uh, affection in her eyes had apparently sidetracked him.

"No, I'm going to ride back with Wibby on the ATV. Brisco can walk you back. You can hold Piper's hand."

Hold Piper's hand? One of Jake's better ideas.

Chapter 8

Piper's phone beeped, and she fished it out of her jeans pocket to check the app. "My roast!" She jogged backward. "Can you tell us whatever it is over dinner? I need to get back ASAP. Just make sure to close the gates behind you! I don't want any more Christmas crias!" She spun and raced toward the first gate.

The roast had to sit for an hour yet, but she needed to get it off the grill. She was bummed that she didn't get to hold Alex's hand back to the house. Really bummed. Before her phone went off, she'd been picturing it in her head: their arms swinging back and forth, their gazes locked on each other, their feet in sync. Silly, but after that second near kiss, she couldn't stop the daydream.

Would his lips ever actually touch hers? Doubtful. And probably best if not. She could get addicted to this handsome, kindhearted man and his sweet son, to this sensation that somehow, right in the middle of her life's mess, she had a reason to celebrate.

Before Alex and Jake came along, she'd wanted to provide that for Libby, even if she didn't feel it herself. But now a real song had started in her heart, one she didn't know the tune to or even how it ended. She shivered.

Why did she always have to think so much when running?

It usually cleared her head, but as she leaped up the steps to the deck, her mind fogged with doubts. Despite their obvious attraction, how could two people in their mixed-up circumstances ever manage beyond friendship?

She grabbed her silicone gloves, lifted the grill lid, and transferred the elk roast pan to the workstation next to the smoker/barbecue. The vegetable dish would stay on longer. This had been Dad's workspace, and Piper felt closer to him every time she used it.

By the same token, she avoided the areas in their home that Mom had considered special, like the craft room. Neither she nor Libby ventured there. A layer of dust probably draped the sewing machine and quilts that filled the room. Mom had stopped going in there much after Dad died, but it was still her spot, and Piper had no desire to feel close to her at the moment.

She was still mad at her, like Libby. But even in her anger, she wished Mom would come home. Just like Libby. She sighed. Why couldn't Mom find herself in Cranberry Creek? Piper had handled her mother's loss by burying her emotions inward and moving forward as best she could. Libby dealt with it by acting out and creating drama. Didn't she realize Piper wished she could just throw a fit sometimes too? No, at fifteen, Libby's world pretty much revolved around herself.

Alex, Jake, and Libby walked up the deck steps at the same time. Alex must have joined them to check on Sophia. Which reminded Piper of their near kiss, even as steam from the roast drifted toward her face.

Just what she dreamed of. The man of her dreams staring at her shiny forehead. It'd probably blind him!

Libby opened the sliding glass door and flipped the light

switch that turned on the chandelier. Dusk had settled, and twilight would soon follow. The starlit sky was far more dazzling out on their country road, away from the artificial lights of the city.

And at twilight, the ranch fun really began. She couldn't wait to treat Alex and Jake to the cria pronking show.

"Wow!" Jake stopped in the middle of the kitchen near the solid-maple table and turned in a slow circle. "I've never been in a ranch house before. It's huge! And it smells so good, wike cookies! Do you have cookies, Wibby? Can I have one?"

"After dinner, Jake," Alex said as he and Piper entered. He was carrying the roast and looked for a place to set it down.

Jake hugged Piper's legs. "Grandma's gone, and Dad only knows how to make tacos. Papa doesn't cook. This is wike what Grandma cooks."

She wrapped an arm around him and snugged him tight against her legs. "I hope you like this." She tried to keep the apprehension out of her voice as she motioned to the granite counter. "Just set it there, Alex. It should rest longer. And I have a show for you guys in a few minutes."

"We're going to watch TV?" Jake asked.

"Nope," Libby said as she opened the stainless-steel fridge. "It's not TV, but it'll be the cutest thing you guys have ever seen. Just you wait."

Piper hunched down in front of Jake. "Do you think you can help Libby with the salad?"

Jake cocked his head. "My dad says salad is just food that real food eats."

"Jake!" Guilt edged Alex's expression.

"It's okay." Piper directed her smirk toward Alex. "You guys don't have to eat it. Libby and I like it though. Do you think you can add the cherry tomatoes to it? And some carrots?"

He skipped over to Libby.

"You're lucky it's a green salad," Libby said, her head in the fridge, "and not quinoa. My sister loves to eat the kind of food that no one can pronounce without practice. The food real food won't eat!"

"What's keen...keen...what?" Jake asked.

Their babble lifted Piper's spirits. Maybe the elk would go over better than she'd thought. She opened the beadboard cupboard and lifted the plates off the shelf. The Franciscan apple design had been her mom's favorite plates, and now Libby refused to eat off them. Piper didn't want to provoke her sister, but paper plates were out of the question tonight. She handed four plates to Alex with one hand while opening the silverware drawer.

"Do you mind?"

He looked at the plates as if he didn't know what to do with them.

Jake wandered up behind him. "Set the table, Daddy. Wike Grandma has me do. Here, I'll show you."

Alex lifted them out of Jake's reach. "You go back to helping Libby. I've got this, Jake."

The interactions resembled that of any normal, happy family. Piper had been much older than Libby, just as Libby was older than Jake. Piper had grown up in this kitchen, hearing conversations like the one taking place between Jake and Alex now.

But she and Libby weren't a happy family. They were two sisters struggling along in a crazy world. Libby deserved more, but all she had was Piper. After Libby was out of college and on her own, maybe Piper could seriously think about a relationship. Unless Mom came home first. Right now, Piper came as a package deal, and who'd want that?

But as she watched the interplay between Jake and Alex—Jake showing Alex how to fold the napkins in half, like "Grandma taught me"—she realized that Alex came as a package deal too, and with his own baggage. His eyes didn't carry that haunted look just because of Jake. She was curious about his late wife, especially after his earlier comment, but that was something he'd have to tell her in his time.

She glanced out the large dining room window. "It's time, guys! Let's go out and watch while the roast is resting."

Libby and the guys filed out behind Piper, where they stood in a line on the deck with a clear view of the paddocks.

"Hey, are they racing?" Jake asked, waving to the romping, prancing crias. "They're all bouncy and happy." He clapped and jumped up and down.

Alex, laughing, held up his phone. "This is too good to miss! I'm recording it."

The crias tore around the paddock and south pasture, weaving in and out among the stoically grazing adults, kicking up grass and hay, pausing occasionally to nudge each other, and then starting all over again.

"It's called *pronking*, and it's showtime nearly every evening at twilight," Piper said. "Their last act before bedding down at night. They will parade around like this for several minutes. And even after all these years, we wait for it every night."

"That is the best roast I have ever had," Alex said as he dipped another bite into the sauce Piper had prepared, some concoction of barbecue sauce, horseradish, and ranch dressing. "So much flavor! Is that from the fancy grill? And these potatoes and carrots—out of this world."

Alex paused as Piper's forehead wrinkled and her eyes showed a bit of hesitation. He'd sensed that in her earlier too. Something was up. Something with the food? With Jake? With Libby?

"Didn't Piper tell you?" Libby asked.

Alex caught her mischievous look as she glanced from Piper to him and back.

"It's elk roast," she said without preamble. "I told Piper you guys were real men, that you'd like it."

Alex almost choked on his bite. He had not been expecting her to say that! The only game he'd ever eaten had tasted...gamey.

"But this is really good," he said after swallowing.

Libby laughed at the surprise in his voice. "My dad hunted, and he knew how to cut meat. You can't cut it anywhere near the bone. That's what gives it a gamey taste. We still have some elk and venison in the freezer. Piper and I grew up on it."

"I wike elk, Daddy," Jake said, as if he ate it all the time. "Can we hunt?"

"Well..." An awkward silence loomed. "I like elk too. But we don't own a gun. And we live in—"

"I know where we wive, Dad. We wive in Seattle. Papa and Grandma used to, but they wive in Cranberry Creek now. We could too." His head swiveled as he looked around the kitchen and dining areas. He leaned back to peer into the great room on the other side of the kitchen peninsula. "This place is big enough for us too. So is Papa and Grandma's."

"Um, Jake..." Could this get any more awkward? "We can't just invite ourselves to live—"

"My dad is flying me to Seattle Friday. You guys wanna come? We have to go to the office. We have a business meeting. We design apps. We're working on a new one. It's about drones."

Saved by his unpredictable son. Alex set his fork down, placed his elbows on the table, and dropped his head onto his palms. Around these two gals, he just never knew what Jake might say or do. Just as Libby had taken the initiative and invited them to dinner, his son had taken the liberty of inviting these beautiful females along on a plane ride. Like that was no big deal. Like they would just hop on a plane to Seattle with them. And since Jake went to work with Alex every day, including business meetings, Jake always talked as if Appstract were his job, his company.

"Can we say it now, Daddy? Can we say it?" Jake bounced around on the booster seat—formerly Libby's.

"Hang on a second." Alex still hadn't told Piper, and he didn't want Jake blurting it out in front of Libby.

"My dad says Appstract is going to sponsor your Christmas party!" Jake announced. "I don't know what sponsor is, but Daddy said it would make Piper happy. Are you happy, Piper?"

This was going from bad to worse. Alex looked up. Libby's narrowed blue eyes reminded him of lava bubbling at the top of a volcano. Piper glanced at Alex questioningly, her hand on Libby's arm, as if to stave off an eruption.

"Jake, I told you it was a secret. I was going to tell you earlier, Piper. I was. But I got..." His gaze inspected her. "Distracted." By his desire to tell her important words on his heart, to kiss her till neither of them could think straight. "But what Jake means is, my company, Appstract, would like to underwrite, or help underwrite, your, uh, the uh—"

"Can you come to Seattle with us on Friday?" Jake interrupted.

"Next Friday, Jake." Alex reined in his frustration before he spoke again. "And I've told you before. Don't interrupt."

"But, Dad—"

"No buts. I'll talk to Piper about the trip and the party. You..." He looked at Libby. Was she really okay? Apparently she'd talked to Jake at the coffee shop about helping with something. She and Alex had chatted a bit about how great Java Creek was, but after that he had tuned out her and Jake's conversation while he tweaked the app on his laptop. Libby had waved a hand in front of his face to get his attention and had invited them to dinner.

Piper scooted her chair closer to Libby's and pulled her sister into a half hug. Libby rested her head on Piper's shoulder.

Explosion averted. Whew! Despite the tension between the sisters, their unmistakable love for each other, their bond, tugged at Alex's heartstrings, and he easily sensed why Jake was so drawn to these two. As an only child, Alex had never experienced a sibling bond, and at this moment, he knew he wanted different for Jake. Just looking at Piper propelled his thoughts in directions he'd never considered. He and Amy had never talked about another child, not after... He wouldn't go there now.

Would Piper want kids? He certainly couldn't ask her this soon! And it didn't matter. Jake was already attached to Libby. Even with all the obstacles in front of them—distance, troubled kids, their emotional baggage—Alex believed he had to do what he could to make sure these sisters didn't disappear from his and his son's lives. He wanted to protect them from life's hurts in the same way he wanted to protect Jake. But he needed to get to know them better first, both of them, so they'd trust him. So Piper would find him worthy. What would she think if she knew about his marriage? Given a second chance at a relationship, Alex vowed he would do it right.

Libby shoved her chair back. "I'll get you a cookie, Jake. We'll let the, uh, grown-ups talk. Besides, I want to show you the yarn I picked out for your hat. And I want to measure your head. Do you want a beanie or a slouchy hat?" She pulled his chair away from the table.

"I don't know what those are. Can you show me on the airplane?"

His son just wouldn't give up!

Chapter 9

Piper steered her Jeep into a parking spot a half mile from Callie's yarn store, Imagknitive. She slung her knitting bag strap over her shoulder as she trekked toward the shop. Vehicles already packed Main Street as the city unleashed its Christmas fervor on this Tuesday after Thanksgiving. Pride for her hometown warmed Piper's insides. She tossed a thumbs-up to the workers who stood on ladders, stringing clear and cranberry-colored LED Christmas lights on the branches of the dormant dogwoods that adorned the sidewalks.

Piper picked up the buzz from tourists and locals wandering through the quaint stores and cafés, the historical-looking facades painted in shades of red, sage, gold, and blue. Several shopkeepers had decorated over the Thanksgiving weekend, some even earlier. Strands of cranberry beads draped from one doorway edge to another and arrayed window frames.

What a difference! When she'd been a kid, many of these storefronts had sat vacant, dilapidated, and cheerless. Libby hadn't ever seen the town in that condition. Piper shivered at the memory of her father wondering what would become of the town his family had ranched in since the early twentieth century. But several wineries had moved into town in the early 2000s, and Cranberry Creek had experienced a revival as central Washington's wine industry boomed. The revitalization continued—intoxicated by the luxurious vineyards that now populated the surrounding hills, city officials had capitalized on the expansion and revamped Main Street. The town had set itself up as *the* holiday destination spot in the Yakima Valley.

She clutched her knitting bag tighter as she recalled her father joining in the town's revival, even laying some of the cobblestone pavers she now walked on, a fact that charmed her every time she meandered the downtown streets. She didn't know if anyone had ever told Libby about her dad and the pavers. She should.

Piper tugged her hat over her ears. Sunny and chilly, a typical prewinter day in the valley. Snow had already fallen heavily in the Cascades, and forecasters were predicting several inches in the valley before Christmas. White Pass Ski Resort had opened over the weekend, and she and Libby had spent Thanksgiving Day snowboarding and ignoring the fact this was their first holiday without either of their parents. Piper had been a little anxious about leaving Sophia in the care of a neighbor who'd farm sat for them. But Emi had assured Piper that Sophia wouldn't deliver until this week or next. Birthing times could be tricky, but Piper trusted Emi, and Sophia hadn't shown any indication she was ready.

Friday, she and Libby had hung out with Sophia in the paddock, knitting their hats right in the shelter while wearing fingerless mitts. Piper had already started decreasing the stitches on her cap. Libby, easily distracted, had barely reached the halfway point on Jake's faux-cable-knit cap.

Somehow, neither of them had ended up at the police station. That fact filled Piper with genuine gratitude. She'd rather see Pete at church than at the PD.

Libby would expect Piper to haul her up to the pass this weekend too. That girl would snowboard every day till the mountain shut down if she could. But with Sophia so close now, they'd miss out this weekend. Piper wouldn't leave Sophia again.

The four downtown wineries dueled it out every Christmas, and their elegant embellishments of garland, lights, mistletoe, wine corks, and cranberry strands captivated Piper's view. She paused under the awning at Sagehill Winery, soaking up a Christmas ambiance she'd thought she'd have to manufacture for Libby's sake. Taking a deep breath, she inhaled the scents of maple bars and sugar cookies wafting from the famous Apple Fritter Bakery next door.

She'd lived in Spokane for five years and had thrived on the energy and bustle of eastern Washington's largest city. But it lacked the warmth, charm, and *coziness* of her hometown, a small city that adored the Christmas season and welcomed a live nativity, a place where store employees wished patrons Merry Christmas and carols played softly from strategically placed street speakers.

This felt like home. This *was* home. Even when Mom returned—if she did—Piper planned to stay. She could illustrate from one of the freelance coworking spaces in Yakima, or open her own coworking space right here in downtown Cranberry Creek. Heck, she could illustrate from a coffee shop if she had to get out of the house.

She regarded the live nativity in the plaza at the center of Main Street. Visions of Jake and Alex, her own sugarplums, danced in her head to the beat of the new melody that had thrummed in her heart ever since she'd met those two city boys. Her own secret carol.

As she stepped from under the winery awning and headed toward Callie's store, she wondered what Alex thought of her hometown. Her chest compressed in a clamp. It surely couldn't compare with the west side of the Cascades, to Seattle's glamor and glitz, or Pike Place Market, the pier, and those spectacular views of Mount Rainier and Puget Sound.

But that could never be Piper's home. Traffic in Spokane had been bad enough. She imagined the crusade every morning in Seattle suburbs to inch onto Interstates 5 and 405. The few times she'd been to Seattle, traffic had been bumper to bumper except maybe at midnight. Granted, the last two times she'd been there for a Mariners game and a Seahawks game. Her dad had loved the Seattle sports teams, pro and semipro. And game-day traffic? The worst.

Cranberry Creek's views included vineyard- and hop-covered hills and apple, pear, and cherry orchards, their pink and white blossoms glorious in the spring, and their verdant fruit-ladened branches and vines spectacular during late-summer and fall harvest. And she couldn't forget the Yakima River and Mount Adams, and even Rainier on clear days.

Other Seattleites had settled here, Piper thought. The valley offered hiking and biking, a lack of traffic, the Yakima River, and the rambling beauty of Cranberry Creek itself, though it might freeze if the weather plunged into the teens.

And hey, it snowed here plenty in the winter and hardly ever rained. In fact, when it wasn't snowing, it was usually sunny. Piper raised her fist to the sky. *Take that, Seattle!*

"What, dear?" asked a thin elderly lady, bundled up in a parka, scarf, and hat, her tiny face barely showing through the layers as she followed a labradoodle on a leash.

Piper paused, covering her mouth with her hand. Had she

said that out loud? She smiled sheepishly. "Just commenting on what a beautiful day it is. I'm sure it's raining in Seattle." Maybe she should drive home and crawl back into bed. Or under a bale of hay.

"I'm sure it is, dear," the woman said. "I don't know why anyone lives there. The weather is so much nicer here." The dog tugged her forward.

Piper would have to try not to go around embarrassing herself any further today.

As she admired the yarn and needle ornaments trimming out the window display at Imagknitive, she reminded herself she might have the opportunity to see where Alex stood on the Cranberry Creek versus Seattle debate when she and Libby flew to the west side with him and Jake. Of course, that wouldn't be for a couple of weeks yet, when Libby was out of school.

The yarn store door flew open, and Callie yanked Piper through the entryway. "Why're you just standing out there staring at my window, girlfriend? It's freezing out there."

Piper stumbled in after her friend, immediately enthralled by the aroma of natural fibers mixed with the gingerbread-and-cinnamon scented candles.

"It's cold all right," Piper said as she slid off her coat. "And sunny. Those clouds only stuck around for a couple of days, and if it doesn't snow soon, Libby will go nuts. She can't wait to drive the tractor around the property. And poor Jake prays for it to snow every day, apparently."

She set her hat and mitts on the large round oak table at the left side of the store, then crossed to where a Keurig coffee maker sat on another table against the wall. She popped an apple cider K-cup into the machine. "What time is everyone supposed to be here, anyway?"

"At three, a half hour," Callie said as she planted her bottom on the table. "Forget about small talk. We can do that later. You sat by Alex and Jake on Sunday again. You so have it bad for that guy." She wiggled her shoulders.

"He goes to your Sunday school class with Jake," Piper protested. "You probably hung around with him as much as I did that day." But Sunday hadn't been the only time she'd seen Jake and his dad since dinner on Tuesday last week.

Alex and Jake had spent several hours on Saturday, helping around the ranch, nailing up plywood, refilling water buckets, and stocking the compost pile. But Callie didn't need to know all that.

"We need to finalize the details for the Kids and Crias event, Callie," Piper said.

"Don't try to change the conversation. We can talk about that when the ladies from church show up to knit hats. I want to know about Alex and Jake. Details, girlfriend. Details." She flipped her blond hair, plopped onto a chair, and patted the seat next to her.

Piper ignored Callie, who apparently lived vicariously through her these days. As vivacious and tenderhearted as Callie was, she didn't date. Ever. It'd take someone special to reach her. Alex might have been that kind of special, but, well, Piper had seen him first.

A display of knitting needles against a side wall near the register snagged Piper's attention. "Hey, you finally got more Dreamz! Took you long enough!" She grabbed a size 10 twenty-inch circ and headed to the table, opening the package as she went. Yes, she had that size already, but only in white-brass needles. She needed this other set too. She did.

And no, she wasn't a needleaholic. Yet. A yarnaholic,

yes. And Callie's support group for yarnaholics only fed the addiction, not curbed it.

She sat in one of the small pleather armchairs Callie had placed around the large round table and slid out her hat project from her knitting bag. "Hi, I'm Piper, and I'm a needleaholic." Okay, so she was a needleaholic. The first step in overcoming her addiction was admitting it, right?

Callie propped her chin against one palm and directed her narrowed gaze on Piper. "You know you're not getting out of this, right?"

Piper sighed. She hadn't knit a single stitch yet today. She would never finish the cap at this rate. She'd be the only one at the event who hadn't finished a single hat.

But she allowed her eyes to twinkle at Callie. "Libby and I are flying with him to Seattle after Sophia has those twins. He invited us for this week, but no way are we leaving Sophia. Hey, you want to come and stay at our place when we go? Can your mom run the shop? Libby and I will water and feed the alpacas Friday morning. Sophia should have given birth. Emi will stay the night, but with her crazy schedule, I can't ask her to do the chores. She'll come and go."

"You don't have to talk me into it! I'll do it, if it means you can go with Alex. *And* if Emi will be around. She's been taking care of your animals for a couple of years. If there's a problem, she'll know what to do." She dropped her palms flat on the table and plunked her chin on her hands. "You're going to Seattle with Alex. How cool is that?"

"Alex is pretty dreamy. He's so kind to me and Libby. And he's amazing with Jake." Piper placed her palms to the table too, matching Callie's pose. "And Jake. He squirmed his way into my heart the second I met him. Libby's too."

She closed her eyes as reality struck a discordant note.

"But seriously, Callie. Libby's hanging on by a thread right now. She's so argumentative, and she's been getting into some big trouble. I hold my breath every time Alex and Jake come around, wondering what she'll do next. I love that girl to pieces, but..." Piper's hands trembled. "She's so tightly wound. But Jake has the most calming effect on her. That kid is kind of addictive." She popped her head up and smiled at Callie... then switched to a frown at her next thought.

"I figure Alex and I don't really stand a chance. And that hurts. He doesn't even live here. And you must have guessed that Jake can't be separated from his dad. We'll never be alone together. And with Libby so volatile... But every time I'm with Alex, my world seems more right, not less right. Even with all the craziness."

"It's a God thing."

Callie wouldn't say that flippantly. Not after everything she'd been through as an abused kid who'd eventually wound up in the home of wonderful Christian foster parents who'd later adopted her. She called that a God thing too.

"I've never seen you like this," Callie murmured, turning her head so her cheek lay on her knuckles. "So happy and scared at the same time. God hears the cries of your heart, Piper. Libby's too. Just as He heard mine." She whispered the last line.

She might have the biggest mouth in central Washington, but sometimes, the sensitive words that came from those lips stunned Piper.

God heard them. Their tears and sorrows, hopes and dreams—they meant something to Him. How often had she really lifted her sister in prayer to Him? Piper promised herself to pray for Libby and with her, at least if Libby allowed her to. They needed comfort from the Comforter.

"But that Libby is an ungrateful brat sometimes."

Uh-oh.

As if energized by her comment, Callie pushed herself from the table, violet eyes ablaze.

"I know she's hurting. How could she not be? But does she realize how lucky she is to have you?"

The shop door dinged and opened, and Mrs. Saunders—Isobel—walked in, Alex and Jake behind her. The three stopped and stared.

Oh dear. Not now, Callie. You were on such a great roll earlier. It's time to close that mouth.

"Callie, umm…"

The door chimed again.

"No!" Callie flung out her arm, completely engrossed in her tirade. "She could've landed in the foster care system, just like I did. It would have been much worse for her. But she has you. You traded your sporty Mazda in for a Jeep, gave up your illustrating career, your apartment, your *life* basically…"

Not all true. Piper still illustrated from home. And she might have returned at some point anyway. But Callie wasn't likely to see reason right now. Piper pressed her fingertips to her forehead. She peeked at Alex and Jake and Isobel and—was that Libby?

"Callie, not everything. You make it sound like—" *Like I'm a saint, and that's so disgustingly far from the truth.*

Piper moaned. This situation had just escalated from bad to worse. She'd forgotten Libby planned to meet them at Imagknitive after school.

"You didn't even hesitate! You dropped everything to take

care of her. You took over running the ranch. Does she know your mom took off with all your dad's life insurance even? That your freelancing helps keep food on your table? That girl needs to hear a piece of someone's mind, and I know just the person to deliver it."

The door slammed, and Libby bolted past the window.

Even Jake didn't call after her that time.

Chapter 10

Callie's head spun toward Alex, Jake, and Isobel, while Piper folded herself into her chair. Alex wondered if he and Jake, and his mom too, should simply back out the door.

"Daddy, is Wibby coming back?" Jake asked. "She told me to come see her today. Remember?"

"Don't worry, Jake." Callie walked to the cash register and grabbed an item out of a wicker basket. She handed him a felted finger puppet. "She'll come back. Look. You can see her."

She pointed out the huge picture window, decorated with yarn balls on ribbon. Battery-operated lights twinkled around some of them.

Jake marched up to the window, and Alex followed him. His mom took a step their direction but then strolled over to Piper.

Jake peered out the window. "She's going to get coffee. Will you text her? I want a strawberry frap."

"Let's let Libby have some space for a minute, buddy."

"Okay."

Before Alex could stop him, he dashed over to Piper, who promptly planted him on her lap.

"Hey, Jake. I, uh, didn't know you guys were coming to knit hats today." She looked at Alex, and despite her friend's rather eye-opening outburst, Piper's joy at seeing him and Jake shone through her chocolate eyes. But she turned them back to his son.

Alex found it so hard to compete with his almost-four-year-old kid. Even Callie gazed at Jake adoringly. She wasn't quite as pretty as Piper, but some would consider her tall form, platinum hair, and violet eyes stunning.

Personally, Alex preferred redheads. With a few freckles. A nicely curved backside. And chocolate eyes he could melt in. The kind of woman who tucked perfectly into his shoulder.

Her lips, heart shaped like her face, bowed up as Jake lifted her needles and yarn in front of him.

"You're silly, Piper. We don't know how to knit. Even Grandma doesn't know. Can you teach her? Daddy says knitting is for girls."

"Your daddy is plain wrong." Callie stomped up to Alex and slugged him on his bicep. "In my store, boys and girls both knit. I'll teach you, Jake."

"But we have to work. Dad said we're going to another coffee shop today. But I wike the one Wibby went to."

Alex didn't miss the puppy-dog look Jake aimed his way, but he was worried Libby might be headed toward an explosion after overhearing Callie's forthright rant. He didn't want himself or his son to trigger it.

"I have an idea," Piper said as Jake scrambled off her lap. "If it's okay with your dad, why don't you two take some time off work, and I'll take a break from knitting, and I'll show you and your dad and grandma the live nativity in the plaza."

"Will Jesus and the shepherds be there?" Jake asked as he reached for Alex's hand. "Can we, Daddy? I really want to see Jesus."

Piper laughed out loud, and the melody of it pealed in Alex's heart, setting off some jingle bells inside of him in response. He tried to think of something witty to say so he could hear it again.

Nothing...he had nothing. He'd probably think of something at 2:00 a.m. though. That was when all his clever lines came to him.

Callie huddled next to Jake. "Remember what I taught you in Sunday school? You know where Jesus lives now?"

"Jesus wives in heaven!"

"Can you see Him with your eyes?"

"No. With my heart." He placed both his hands on his chest.

"You remembered! You're a good kid, Jake. So what you see out there isn't the real Jesus, okay?"

"Okay."

Oh, the faith of a child.

"Can we go see the fake baby Jesus, Dad?"

That brought another melodic laugh from Piper, and Alex's heart responded with its own harmony. At least his son could be witty.

"I think I'll stay right here where it's warm and cozy," his mom said. "You kids go ahead. I want to learn to knit, and a few other women from church will be here before long."

Callie straightened. "Yeah, go ahead, 'you kids.'" She slanted a grin their way. "Just be back at four, Piper. We'll plan the Kids and Crias event down to the last detail once everyone's here."

Piper—the woman Alex's mom had referred to as his girlfriend this morning—shoved her yarn and needles into her bag and set it against a wall. She settled her cap on her head and slipped on her mittens. When she neared Jake, she reached for his hand, an automatic gesture. Alex still held Jake's other hand.

Alex longed to spend time alone with this sweetheart of a woman, maybe wandering onto the walking bridge over the creek on the other side of town or strolling with her hand in his through this charming downtown in the midst of decking itself out for the season.

But he'd take what he could get.

Piper would never be so bold as to hold Alex's hand in front of everyone, but she swung Jake's arm lightly, noting that Alex did the same with Jake's other arm.

"Hey, wook. There's Wibby." Jake let go of their hands and darted a few steps in front of them. He waved his hands. "Wibby. Wibby. We're over here."

From across the street, Libby's head lifted as she zeroed in on Jake. She carried a tray full of drinks.

Piper kept Libby's Java Creek card with enough of a balance so Libby could order there pretty much anytime. She supposed she was spoiling her just as Mom had. But she'd probably have to up the balance if Libby intended to buy for Jake and Alex regularly.

Alex, as if not even thinking about it, reached for Piper's hand. The heat traveled from his hand right along the nerve that pathed straight to Piper's heart. The zing to that vital organ surely took years off her life. Or maybe added them.

It was worth it either way.

He didn't let go of her, even when Libby breezed across the street.

Piper tensed, and Alex squeezed her hand tighter.

Hopefully, those drinks in Libby's hand wouldn't end up on Piper's head. She loved this hat. Surely Libby wouldn't make that much of a scene.

When she stopped in front of them, Libby glanced up with... was that regret in her eyes? Had what Callie said actually meant something to her? Piper squinted at her sister. Yeah, and there might be something more there too.

Maybe gratefulness?

No, she was daydreaming now. She glanced down. Alex was holding her hand for real, in front of Libby and Jake and Mrs. Appleton from church, who waved a hi as she hefted her paisley knitting bag and entered Imagknitive.

Libby stood on the cobblestone pavers she didn't know Dad had helped lay and handed Jake a kid-sized cup.

"Here, Jake. I thought you might like to try this candy-cane frap. I know you love fraps.

"And Alex, a large holiday blend for you, black."

Alex took his drink without releasing Piper's hand.

"And Piper, your holiday favorite."

This was as close as Libby would get to apologizing. Piper gladly accepted it. She didn't need the actual words.

"Smoked toffee, extra whip." Libby swayed the cup under Piper's nose.

The sweet aroma went straight to Piper's head. She'd forgive just about anything for a sip of that concoction.

"Your first one for the season," Libby chimed. "I know, because Jessica said they just started making them today."

Jessica was Libby's favorite barista and was usually on duty after school let out.

"We're going to see the fake baby Jesus, Wibby. Wanna come?" Jake asked

Libby giggled and extended her arm toward the boy, but her gaze embraced Piper, who stood amazed at her sister's almost humble attitude. Piper relaxed her fingers, still gripping Alex's. She'd take Libby at face value. She seemed genuinely glad, at least at the moment, that she had a big sister.

It was enough.

"Of course Libby wants to come," Piper said, her eyes embracing her sister in return.

And without Jake even realizing it, though his father certainly did, the boy swept Libby's hand into his and trooped ahead of Alex and Piper.

She felt the indrawn breath of the man beside her.

Alex's eyes locked on to hers. The emotion swirling in those flecked hazel depths matched the tumult clenching her stomach. His grip tightened, and he twirled Piper toward him as her sister and his son wandered obliviously in front of them.

"I've been wanting to do this since the day I walked onto your ranch and you knelt in front of my son. My heart attached to yours in an instant. I know you didn't feel it..."

Oh, he couldn't be more wrong about that.

"...but I haven't been able to stop thinking about you. About us. I know it's crazy. We can't even take a walk alone together. I promise to get help for me and Jake when we get home after New Year's. But I don't know when I'll get another opportunity for this, and I'm sorry we're not alone and somewhere more romantic—"

She placed a finger on his lips. *Just shut up and kiss me already, before another lady from church pulls up!*

He dipped his head. Piper closed her eyes and waited for someone to interrupt them. For someone to chastise her for her boldness.

She wouldn't have heard them anyway. The pounding of her heartbeat would have drowned them out.

His lips melted into hers, hungry but reserved. She welcomed them, eager but restrained, returning in full measure. Right there in downtown Cranberry Creek. Yet even as Alex deepened the kiss and crushed her to his chest, she sensed his withdrawal. And his regret. He separated their lips with air—*oh please, not yet*—and rested his chin on her stocking cap.

She inhaled deeply, trying to control her surging heart rate and emotions, her desire for more.

"Someday I hope to do that without an audience," Alex mumbled into her hat. "Then you'll know how a guy from the west side really kisses a girl from the east side."

Piper laughed into his neck. "Yeah, well, we east-side girls give as good as we get, so that will be an experience you won't forget."

Alex groaned and cupped the back of her head, tucking it more securely into his shoulder.

A thrill jolted through Piper, but she squelched it resolutely. The possibility of that happening anytime soon was nil. And that was probably a good thing, she thought as his arms loosened. But she'd happily settle for even a few minutes alone just to *talk* to him without the anticipation they'd be interrupted at any second.

"We'd better catch up to those kids, or they'll figure out what we're up to."

Alex rotated her, and they aimed their bodies in the direction of their responsibilities. Libby's finger pointed to the manger at the downtown park, and Jake lurched forward slightly to get a better view.

This time, it wasn't Jake who turned around, but Libby. She watched them over her shoulder.

Alex wasn't holding Piper's hand. He'd anchored his arm around her.

Libby halted Jake to wait for them to catch up, a knowing look in her glance.

A dissonant twang filtered into the melody in Piper's heart.

How did two people who could never be alone manage to discover each other's hopes and dreams?

But when Piper viewed Jake, she could see straight into Alex's heart. This man had sacrificed a great deal for the benefit of a son who'd lost his mother. And he'd promised to get help for Jake's separation anxiety.

But what could she alter in her relationship with Libby in order to strengthen her bond with Alex?

Chapter 11

Jake banged the Transformer action figure into the plastic dragon and crashed the two toys against the stone fireplace with a loud "Fire! Fire! Get out!"

"Jake, you'll wake up Grandma. I told you to keep it down." Alex sat on the leather love seat with his bare feet propped against the rustic pine chest that served as a coffee table, his computer on his lap. He supposed he should change out of his flannel pajama bottoms. Jake would grumble about taking off his beloved fleece Transformer pj's, which he'd wear all day if Alex would let him. Which he'd done once. A huge mistake. Jake had then wanted to wear them to the office.

"But, Dad, the city's on fire." Jake picked up two other figures and dashed them against the metalwork arch surrounding the fireplace doors. "Besides, it's almost wight out. Grandpa's outside stacking wood. And Grandma plays with me."

True. Mom was great with Jake. In the weeks they'd been here, she'd really bonded with him. When Amy was alive...she hadn't wanted to travel, and his parents' visits had been tense and brief.

Jake was close buds with his grandpa now too. Alex knew his dad wished he could do guy stuff with Jake without Alex around all the time, and Alex hoped that day would come sooner rather than later.

As close as Jake was becoming to his grandma, his bond with Libby was even tighter. And even with Piper, he showed almost no reserve. Alex placed his hand over his heart and let his head rest on the back of the love seat as a pterodactyl zoomed toward the coffee table.

He'd kissed her yesterday. On a busy street. In front of the whole town. That was the best he could do right now, since there was zero chance he'd be alone with her, even for talking. The sweet smiles she directed his way, her tenderness with Jake, her willingness to sacrifice for Libby...it all simply added up to someone he was falling in love with. There weren't a lot of women like her. And despite the tension between Piper and Libby, Alex sensed that deep down the teenager was a wonderful girl. Her feelings and actions toward his son, and him too, were genuine. She liked him; he liked her. And Piper was doing her best with her. He'd support her in that however he could.

But Piper. He'd never been truly alone with her, and how long could she put up with that? Having a kid around nonstop was absolutely exhausting. Would that same amazing character trait that led her to give up so much for Libby allow her to move forward in a relationship with Alex?

Could he even ask that of her?

Not right now, he couldn't.

Please, Lord. I know I'm not where I should be spiritually. But I have no doubt that You placed Piper and Libby in our lives, in my life, for a reason. Show me the next step with her and the right steps to take to help Jake and me get ourselves on the right course.

"Comin' at ya, Dad!"

A T. rex crashed into Alex's legs, and he lifted them so Jake could crawl under.

He snapped his laptop closed. He'd hardly been able to list the simplest task this morning on the drone app. It was a clever concept—pinpointing drones in the app user's vicinity. The design would be complex and was in the early planning stages, but visions of a redhead with a ponytail and a knit cap were disrupting Alex's attempts to determine the app's core functions.

"I still don't get it, Dad." Jake's head popped up on the other side of the coffee table.

Alex didn't even have to ask what Jake meant. His kid had gone on all morning—they'd been up since 5:30—asking why Piper and Libby couldn't stay at the condo when they flew to Seattle with Jake and Alex after Libby's school let out for the holidays.

Alex had mentioned to his mom last night that he'd booked the sisters a room at Belltown Inn, just a few blocks from his condo and the office in the trendy Seattle neighborhood he and Jake had moved to after Amy had died. Alex hadn't wanted to commute from his and Amy's Shoreline home once he had to cart Jake to work with him every day. On a good day, Shoreline was only twenty or so minutes from downtown Seattle, but the drive often took more than an hour.

"Our place has wots of room."

No, it didn't. It was a small condo. But it had great views of Puget Sound and the Olympic Mountains, scenes Alex never tired of.

One of Jake's little eyebrows pointed up and the other inched down, his serious look. Alex couldn't figure out how he managed it. Once Jake dug in his heels, he didn't let go. No matter what. And he was determined that Libby and Piper would stay with them.

"I thought maybe we'd take them to the Olympic Sculpture Park," Alex said.

Okay, that had been calculated to distract Jake, who loved to make up stories about the edgy, abstract sculptures.

"It doesn't wook wike an eagle, you know, Dad." His eyes lit up.

He could go on and on about that sculpture. He was convinced that Calder's *Eagle*, arguably the best-known sculpture of the park, was actually a dinosaur.

Alex silently thanked Alexander Calder for his genius.

"I wike eating wunch at the park. Can Wibby and Piper eat there with us?"

"Sure, buddy. That's a great idea. We can if it's not raining." Alex rose and set his laptop on the cushion beside him as a beam of early sunlight streamed through the window. He could get used to the bright mornings here. Usually, he and Jake walked to work in a gray, drizzly shroud, even in the summer, though the afternoon sun created breathtaking shimmers on Puget Sound and exposed the majesty of Rainier to the south and the Olympic Mountains to the west. Didn't happen a lot in the winter though.

"Come on. Let's go get you some hot chocolate."

With Bumble Bee clutched in one hand and a brontosaurus in the other, Jake dashed ahead of him into the kitchen.

Wednesday had perched the sun high and bright on a below-freezing morning. Alex noted the twenty-five-degree temperature on the large outdoor thermometer his dad had placed on a blue spruce in the backyard.

Alex stuck a Junior Mint chocolate K-cup in the coffee machine on the quartz counter. Ever since they'd arrived, Mom had been spoiling Jake with hot chocolate every morning and homemade huckleberry pancakes for breakfast—Jake's favorite. The kid was sure going to miss Grandma when they drove home for good after New Year's.

A pang flitted through Alex's chest as he set Jake's mug on the rustic kitchen table and lifted him onto the booster seat he'd insisted Alex buy after Jake had sat on Libby's old one at dinner there last week. Before that, he'd been happy with a couple of phone books.

Alex pried the action figure and dinosaur from Jake's fingers. "No playing with toys at the table." He set them on the counter.

As Alex lowered the coffee machine lid onto his own pumpkin spice K-cup, he thought how the charms of Seattle, even his condo's stunning views, paled when compared to the sparkle of a redhead who lived on this side of the state.

"I know, Dad. Wibby could sleep on the couch."

He just wouldn't let it go.

"And Piper could sleep in the other bedroom. Hey, can I have marshmallows in my hot chocolate? Grandma always puts marshmallows in my cup. And whip cream."

He was so easily distracted...

"What? She never put whipped cream in my chocolate when I was growing up!"

"That's 'cause you're not a grandkid." Mom grinned at him as she padded into the kitchen in her pink terry cloth bathrobe. She opened the pantry, unclipped a bag of mini marshmallows, and plopped a few into Jake's mug.

Alex picked out a K-cup for his mom and pushed brew. Then he opened the fridge and handed her the whipped cream.

"Dad won't wet Wibby and Piper stay at our condo, Grandma."

"I know, Jake," she said as she squeezed a dollop of whipped cream into his cup. She sat across from him and accepted a mug of coffee from Alex. "We talked about that last night. It's better for them to stay at a hotel. Maybe you can have breakfast with them at the hotel restaurant."

"But we have enough room. I need more marshmallows, Grandma."

Alex caught the direct look she aimed his way as she plunked a few more mini marshmallows into the whipped-cream swirl. She'd wanted to talk to him last night, he knew, but he'd spent some time reading on his iPad after Jake had fallen asleep at 8:30. He was trying, with his pastor's encouragement, to read through the New Testament by Christmas, but he was only to 2 Peter. He'd need to pick up the pace to meet his goal.

"We're going to take our coffee into the family room, Jake," Alex's mom said. "You can see us from the table. I want you to drink your chocolate here."

"I won't spill," he said, starting to slide off the booster.

"Listen to Grandma, Jake," Alex said. "You can come in as soon as you finish your drink."

"Can I play with my Transformers at the table?" He shifted to center himself again.

"Just this once," Alex said as he handed them to him.

He followed his mom into the family room. She sank into one of the club chairs opposite the love seat and motioned for him to sit. She retrieved her knitting project for the Criations Kids and Crias event from the basket on the floor and set it on her lap.

"They cast on for me at the store and showed me how to knit and purl, and that's all I'm doing right now. Making the ribbing for the hat." But she didn't pick up her needles.

Bummer.

The determined set of her jaw informed Alex there was no way he was getting out of this conversation. But he'd at least try.

"Maybe Jake and I should go help Dad stack wood, and you can knit in peace," Alex said as he set his mug on the coaster on the trunk between them.

"You know he doesn't want help," she said. "He didn't even want you to chop it. He's not even fifty yet, Alex. Just sit your butt down." She pointed to the love seat.

He sighed but complied. "Keep your voice a little low. I don't want Jake hearing more than he has to."

"He has his chocolate and his toys. He'll be fine."

Alex wished he'd refilled his cup before leaving the kitchen. He might need the extra support a full mug of caffeine could provide.

"That Piper is someone special," Mom said.

She always did get right to the point. Jake had the same tendency.

"I know, Mom. I can't get over how amazing she is. She runs that ranch, wrote that book, is organizing this Christmas event, and makes time for her sister. And even me and Jake. She's sweet but strong. Other than you, I didn't even realize there were women of her caliber out there." He rubbed a hand along the back of his neck, which had heated. He didn't usually speak to his mom like that.

Sure, since he'd moved to Belltown, women had hinted around, had even asked him out in front of Jake. They seemed like nice enough career-minded gals, and that was great. He had no problem with that. But because of his son, he hadn't even considered going out with any of them. And they were mere candles compared to the torch Piper lit inside him. She understood about Jake. She welcomed his son into her life. As did her sister. Not a one of those other women had ever hunched to Jake's level.

"But she's not perfect, and she's having a hard time with that sister of hers. I saw them at church regularly before Paul, their father, died."

She had a full cup of coffee—plenty of fortification before she made her next point. Which might be a doozy, because she took a long sip and kept her hands wrapped around her mug.

"They seemed like such a great family, but when Paul died, Angela, their mom, lost track of herself, stopped coming to church. Got into yoga to help her deal with the stress. And I'm not saying that part is bad, of course, but then she fell into the whole Eastern philosophy thing and seemed to lose herself in it. Libby came to church for a while with the youth group, but she eventually stopped too. And then Angela took off. Has Piper told you any of this?"

Alex set his elbows on his knees but kept his eyes on his mom. Piper had filled him in on a few details as they'd wandered in the downtown plaza yesterday. Which led his mind directly to their kiss, just as sweet as the rest of her. His pulse spiked at the mere thought of it. But he couldn't think about that in front of his mother, that was for sure.

"Not all of it, no. Of course, I know her mom left and that she came home to take care of Libby and the alpaca ranch. She doesn't think her mom will return anytime soon. I figured the rest would come out in time. I tell her stuff whenever there's an opportunity, and she does the same." He flashed a mischievous grin. "Jake's a tad demanding, and Libby is... I worry about saying or doing something that will set her off. But she's a good kid, I promise, Mom. Just a little mixed up right now, and with good reason."

"Of course she has reason! I'm not implying otherwise." She set her cup on a coaster and tapped nervous fingertips together. She tightened the belt on her robe.

"Piper makes sure Libby's at the youth group every week and in church on Sundays. She's providing a solid foundation for her sister. I don't know her well, but I'm proud of her. Bottom line here, son, is that I don't want to see those girls, or you or Jake, get hurt. Jake talks about them nonstop, and you...it's clear how you feel about Piper already. But the last thing they need is someone else they're close to leaving them. And what about Jake? He's going to miss Libby and Piper something fierce already. And if the two of you ever move forward in a serious relationship, what would you do about Jake? He still sleeps in a room with you! And you and Piper don't even live on the same side of the Cascades!"

"I know I live in Seattle, Mom." Now he sounded petulant, like Jake. "I've already started the process to get us help as soon as Jake and I get back to Seattle after the holidays." He brushed shaking fingers through his messy hair, the gel from yesterday making it flop heavily on his forehead.

He wondered if he even wanted to return to Seattle permanently. He hadn't spent much time east of the Cascades before this, just a week or so every two or three years growing up, but the slower pace, the vineyards and orchards, the rolling hills, and this charming town offered a serenity that was missing in his life. Not to mention the support of his parents and Piper and Libby with Jake.

But could he and his son get help here, in the Yakima Valley? With something as serious as this?

"You and Jake are welcome to stay here as long as you like, you know. And Yakima has a great children's medical center, Children's Village."

Had she read his mind?

"I'm just noting that…just in case… Anyway, the *Yakima Herald-Republic* has run several articles on the place in the last few years. It's known nationwide for its work with children. I'm just throwing it out there."

"I know. Just in case."

"One last thing."

Jake dropped his forehead into his palms. He'd hoped that was the last of it.

"Have you talked to Piper about Amy yet?"

Alex cleared his throat. Twice. He lifted his mug to his lips, but he found only the bottom of the cup. Did she have to know everything? Moms!

With dad it was like, *How you doin', son?*

Fine. Everything's great.

You like that Piper gal a lot, huh?

Yeah, I think I do.

Glad to hear it.

And that was it. But moms—they asked questions!

"She knows my wife died. I've told her a little bit…a little about our marriage. Not enough."

"She needs to know, son."

"We're going over there later today to help her get a couple of trees. We're going to drive up to Cliffdell, to Dad's friend's property off Highway 410. Libby will probably fuss about the trees—she doesn't think they should celebrate Christmas without their mom—but I think Piper really wants them. One for the barn and one for the house. When Libby gets home from school, she'll probably entertain Jake. I'll tell Piper then."

"You need to—"

Jake charged into the family room and launched himself onto his grandma's lap. "I wooked out the window and saw a cloud!"

Indeed, the sunbeam had disappeared from the wood floor.

Alex's mom tickled Jake's sides, and he wiggled and laughed, a sound that never failed to stir Alex.

Jake had been on cloud patrol ever since Libby had promised him, crossed her heart even, that it would snow in Cranberry Creek.

Chapter 12

Piper hated to fight with her sister before she caught the bus for school, but her level of obnoxiousness this morning raised Piper's ire. She'd just wanted to snuggle into the overstuffed rocker recliner and knit a little more on the second hat she'd started for a foster kid before she headed back out to the animals.

"We aren't getting a Christmas tree!" Libby said again as she stomped from the mudroom to the family room, one UGG boot in her hand. "Not without Mom. You promised, Piper. Hey, do you know where my other boot is?" She dropped her boot on the barnwood floor and slid her foot in.

Piper set her project onto the arm of her chair, hoping she didn't wind up strangling Libby with the yarn.

She checked the water kettle on the black woodstove. She needed to keep her mouth shut a few seconds before she responded to the Christmas tree remark. She'd thought they'd argued it to death last night, but Libby had hopped out of bed this morning swinging the same stick.

The burn ban had lifted a couple days ago, so Piper was enjoying a real fire in the woodstove. She'd probably have to let the fire go out in the next day or so as the clouds blanketed the sky, but for now, she could keep the furnace off and heat the farmhouse with the woodstove. That would save a bit on their extraordinary monthly heating bill.

She thanked God for the woodpile her dad had kept stocked, chopping cord after cord of tamarack every spring and summer. With the frequent burn bans, it'd still take them a couple months to finish off the last of it. Some of the bigger rounds still needed splitting, and Piper figured if she could pitch hay, she could chop wood. That was one thing Dad had always done. Not Piper or Libby or Mom, ever. But she'd figure that out when the time came.

"You can't just ignore me and think I'll go away," Libby said as she lifted a pile of clean laundry off one end of the cinnamon-colored sectional.

Actually, I can. You'll be leaving to catch the bus in just a couple of minutes.

"Your boot's not on the couch, Libby!" Piper tromped toward the mudroom, opened the pine shoe chest, dug around, and pulled up Libby's other boot. She marched back into the family room.

"You keep work boots in your bedroom and UGGs in the mudroom?"

Libby snatched the boot out of her hand. "Thanks. Don't change the subject. We're still not getting a tree. I said I'd help with the Kids and Crias thing you insist on doing..."

At this point, kiddo, I don't even care what you want.

"...but I don't see why we have to decorate in the house. That's always something we did when you came home for the weekend, and we..." Her voice blipped as she pulled her fleece sweatshirt on over her black tank top. She sank to the floor and grabbed her other boot, but she just sat there with it in her hand. "I just...can't imagine doing this without Mom. Maybe she'll come home in time for Christmas. And then we can..."

The heat deflated out of Piper, and she flopped beside Libby. Neither believed that would happen.

She leaned her head on Libby's shoulder, and Libby rested her cheek on Piper's hair.

"But it's still Christmas, Libby. And Alex and Jake are coming over tonight. And Alex is willing to take me to Cliffdell to cut down two big trees...some place his dad knows about. We'll get a tall one for the vaulted ceiling in here. You don't have to go with us. I need you to stay here and keep an eye on Sophia. And I'll get up every two hours and check on her through the night."

"Piper...it just doesn't feel right."

She and Jake were a lot alike. When she got an idea in her head, she just wouldn't let it go.

"Besides, it'll be nearly dark when you get up there."

"There will be plenty of light left. And Alex and Jake will help us decorate. Besides, Alex is bringing stuff to make tacos for dinner."

"I still don't like it," Libby whined. "But Jake is so cute. Do you think he'll ride on the ATV after what happened last time?"

Piper just nodded, her hair scuffling against Libby's cheek. She recalled the promise she'd made to herself about praying more for Libby other than just mealtimes. She hadn't followed through. Yet.

She shuffled a bit and sat cross-legged.

"Libby, I...I want to pray with you. Can we do that?"

Libby tugged on her other boot and sat in the same position opposite her sister.

Piper held Libby's hands in hers. Libby probably

didn't realize it, but she'd given Piper a gift with her silent acquiescence.

Piper bowed her head. She didn't check if Libby did the same. It was okay if she didn't. "Dear Father, You know our hurting hearts. We just lift our mom up to You. We pray You'd keep her safe, that You'd reach her heart and restore her to fellowship with You, with us."

The squeeze of Libby's fingers bolstered Piper. "I pray a special blessing on Libby today, that You'd comfort her in the way only You can, that the love of Jesus would soothe her."

"And, Lord..."

Pipers fingers clamped around Libby's when she spoke. Her sister was praying!

"Please help Sophia to deliver healthy twin crias. It would mean so much."

Why hadn't Piper thought to pray that?

"And thank you for a sister who puts up with my crap, who doesn't give up on me. Amen."

Piper sighed. She supposed God had heard worse.

Libby jumped to her feet. "Great RT, sis. Love ya. I'm outta here." She grabbed her backpack and ran out the back door without closing it.

Yeah. Great RT—real talk. Just great.

A second later, Libby popped her head back into the family room from the door she hadn't shut. "Oh! And we are still not getting a tree!" This time she slammed the door.

Piper rather wished she'd just gone ahead and strangled her with the yarn.

Sophia's ears twitched forward as Piper palmed her some

grain. The dam had been staying close to the shelter, and her humming picked up in frequency too whenever Piper checked on her. Sure signs that delivery was just around the corner.

Piper had set up a pen in the barn for her, with access to a small paddock. She coaxed Sophia with some grain to the barn paddock, where Fresca and Dominique already grazed.

"You ready to move in?" she asked as she walked Sophia down the laneway. "I've prepared a special place for you to welcome your crias into the world. I know you'd like a sunny day for giving birth, but you're running out of those. You might have to settle for some clouds. And maybe even snow."

Since Sophia had made it this far, Piper's optimism abounded that both crias would live. And Libby had staked the tent of her hopes on their survival, as if that could somehow make up for Mom taking off. But given the rarity of such a birth, not even the vet knew what the possibility of survival was.

"You'll be such a brilliant, nurturing mommy to Mikko and Pikko," Piper cooed. "We're going to take good care of you. Give you lots of grains and herbs so you have enough milk. We have special coats for your crias. Emi says you'll be famous, that the TV and newspapers will be out here to write stories about you and your babies. Real stories this time. I might even write another book. And we have about twenty kids coming to see you and them just before Christmas. Your beautiful crias will be like a Christmas present to them."

The women from church and Callie's shop had already finished ten hats for the kids. They had started knitting and crocheting as soon as Piper and Libby had asked them to participate. Even Isobel had committed to finishing one. Every child in the families coming for the event would receive a cap, whether a foster child or a natural one.

"And Jake, he'll be thrilled. Libby will be beside herself. And Emi might even get her own story or two. Isn't she the best vet ever? She's such a good friend. I adore her."

In fact, Emi had just left after looking Sophia over and determining that the birth would happen in the next two or three days.

"Piper, Piper, we're here!" Jake's voice drifted from the chestnut tree.

Piper waved him over to the barn paddock. "Sophia's been waiting to see you guys all day!" Of course, she really meant *she* had been waiting all day. She'd struggled through her two illustrating projects that morning—her distracted mind had been busy sketching a visual of Alex's hazel eyes and scruffy jawline, and it hadn't been long till her hands had found a blank page in her sketch pad. *And then I had the nerve to pencil myself in beside him. Like a teenage girl. Only worse. I used more hearts around our portrait.*

Because I think…I think…I might be falling in love with him already.

"Where's Wibby?" Jake asked as he hurled himself toward Piper.

The real question was, where was Alex? She scanned the fence and yard and driveway. Alex leaned against his pickup, one leg bent at the knee and crossed at the ankle, observing Piper and Jake. But Jake didn't look over once to see where his father was.

She raised her arm and fluttered her fingers at Alex. She'd let him have a private moment, considering how precious few of those he must have.

"She's in the house making something special for you. And

you just missed the vet, my good friend Emi. She said Sophia will probably have her twins by the end of the week."

He pulled off one glove—was that a child-sized work glove?—and reached into the grain bag Piper held.

"I can't wait to see Mikko and Pikko," he said to Sophia, his palm flat. "They're going to be so pretty, just wike you. I'm going to help take good care of them." He dropped his hands to his sides, scrunched, and sloped forward. Sophia tilted her nose down for a kiss.

He speaks to her just as Libby or I would.

Jake patted one of his legs and stuck out one foot. He grabbed her hand. "Wook at my pants and boots. Dad bought me Carts...Car..."

"Carhartts."

"Carhartts. And boots with a flap, just like Wibby's. So I can help more on the farm. So I can help with the Christmas party."

"And look at that spiffy work jacket." Piper plucked him on the elbow. "You look like a real ranch hand now."

Alex sauntered forward, tweaked her ponytail, and pulled her into a one-armed embrace. She felt the whisper of a kiss on her ear warmer just as Libby charged through the gate toward them, her blond hair bouncing on her own shoulders.

"Hey, you two. I saw that, Alex! None of that!" she said. "Jake, come here."

She held out an arm, but Piper shifted Jake out of Libby's reach. *He's just fine here beside me. She doesn't have to hog him.*

"I'm just going to ignore that," Alex said as he folded his other arm around Libby and side-hugged her as well.

"And look at you, Jake!" Libby exclaimed.

Piper relinquished his hand as he moved toward her sister.

"You're all decked out, just like a real alpaca farmer. Wow," she said as she bent and kissed his cheek. "Are you totally ready to ride the ATV with me to fill the water buckets? These dams and sires and crias need warm water."

"Will Brisco stay with my dad and Piper?" His expression puckered.

If Jake didn't ride off with Libby, then Alex would have the best reason ever not to explain to Piper about Amy. About how he'd made mistake after mistake. But if he didn't tell her, then how could he assure her he wanted to do things right this time? And what if when she found out, what if she dropped him like—

"Hey, Brisco," Libby called. "Come here, pup!"

Pup? That dog must weigh more than a hundred pounds. Brisco trotted toward Libby, who ran with Jake to open the proper gates. When they returned, Alex scanned Jake's eyes for real panic. But his son didn't seem nervous, just in need of reassurance.

"Jake, if you'd rather stay here with me and Piper—"

"I want to go with Wibby!"

For once when Alex needed him glued to his side, Jake was Goo Gone.

The Great Pyrenees halted and sat by Jake, who plowed his face into Brisco's neck.

"Will you take care of my dad and Piper?"

Brisco sidled his head, as if he understood.

"He'll watch you, Daddy. He wistened to me." And with that, Jake put his other glove back on and stuck his hand out for Libby to take.

"Love those work gloves," she said. "Those will come in handy when we're lifting the buckets."

"Yeah, and Dad bought me snow gloves too. I see clouds, Wibby. Maybe after it snows we can build a snowman..."

Alex could picture Jake doing this every day. Visiting the farm, Piper and Libby. Spending time with his grandparents. They had filled a security void in Jake's young life and heart. He soaked up the atmosphere and attention like the desert soil here soaked up water. The support nourished the boy's young soul.

His wasn't the only one.

Now how, Lord, do I tell this girl that I've only just found my footing with You and that I royally messed up with Amy?

Alex snugged Piper to his chest for a fleeting second and then released her. "Okay, what's up for today? Do we have bales of hay to break up? Shelters to layer? A barn to clean? Poop to scoop?"

"Oh, city boy thinks he can handle a pitchfork, does he?"

She took off her gloves and shoved them into her pockets. With her right hand, she gripped his left wrist. She traced his palm with the fingertips of her other hand—she was also a lefty, he'd noted days ago—just below his fingers, over the callus that had formed when he'd chopped Piper's wood two days ago. *So there!*

"Okay, okay, I've never even touched a pitchfork before, but how hard can it be?" He'd held her hand several times now and remembered only silky delicateness, his hand dwarfing hers. But being left handed, he'd always reached for her right hand. If he examined her dominant hand, would he find traces of how hard she must work on this farm?

"Wouldn't want to ruin that manicure." She winked as she

released him. “Lucky you, I did all that before you came. I was hoping you might want to walk to the creek at the north side of our property. We’ll be within Jake’s view the whole time, unless they stop at a paddock shelter or the barn.” She twirled her ponytail tightly, her head bound only in a knit—what did she call it? Ear warmer? “I thought it would just be fun to walk and talk. But when I say it like that, it sure doesn’t sound exciting.” She let her ponytail pop out of the swirl and flicked her fingers over it again.

Alex stilled her hand with his. What if she kept twisting until it all unwound from her head? He plucked her hand from her copper mane and clutched it in his.

“A walk sounds perfect. So tell me,” he said as he matched his footsteps to hers, lightly swinging their arms between them. “How did the creek get its name? Do they grow cranberries in the Yakima Valley? I don’t recall that they do. As a kid, I didn’t care enough to ask. Never thought about it even.”

Piper laughed as she motioned with her other hand for Brisco to follow them. “That’s one of the crops we *don’t* grow here! They prefer bogs. But when we get to the creek, if you can wait that long, I’ll show you where the name comes from.”

“I’ve taken Jake to see it where it runs through my parents’ property, but there’s no path that leads directly to the water there. We just view it from a distance. I could see a reddish hue along the shore. I keep meaning to ask my parents, but I’ve been interrupted so many times, I’ve never gotten the question out.”

Alex shaded his eyes with his forearm as they neared the creek. Clouds streaked the horizon, the sun behind them painting a hazy orangish-red behind the surrounding hills and Mount Adams.

From this vista, it looked as if the creek ran directly in front of the mountain.

"Your view here is incredible," he said.

"It is great! If it were more clear, you'd see the tip of Rainier from here. It's one of my favorite viewing spots.

"There're some great trails for the Mount Adams wilderness area on the Yakama Indian Reservation." She paused her voice, but her feet continued forward. "Sometime, maybe, uh, maybe I...I don't know if you hike, but maybe I could take you on a trail."

"I haven't hiked in years. I'm totally out of practice. But I'd love to take that hike with you." He figured he'd carry Jake if he had to. He'd better start working out more.

"Come over here along the creek." She started down a short path. "Wait. Jake can still see us from here, but that might dip low enough to be out of his line of sight. Stay right there. I'll be right back."

Alex perched himself on a boulder away from a clump of trees to be sure he stayed within Jake's sight. Brisco sat sentry beside the rock.

Piper reappeared, and one hand fisted.

"Scoot over. You're hogging the only spot worth sitting on along the entire creek."

Alex shifted toward the center, taking up even more of the boulder.

"Uh-uh, bud. Not sitting on your lap. If you want to see what's in my hand, make room."

"Gotta give a guy credit for trying," he grumbled as he moved his knees aside.

She landed beside him and held out her closed fist, fingers side up. One by one, she unfolded them to reveal...cranberries?

"The look on your face! Priceless!"

She laughed as he picked up one of the "berries" and examined it.

"It's actually a pebble. The shoreline of this creek is lined with these cranberry-colored pebbles, and when the town revamped itself back in the early 2000s, when the wineries started locating here, it made this its signature color and set itself as the holiday destination in the valley. My dad played a part in renovating the town."

Alex gathered the rest of the pebbles in her hand and slipped them into his pocket.

"It's illegal to harvest them. They put a stop to that way back in the mid-nineteen hundreds."

"I promise I'll bring them back someday," he said. "I'm not harvesting them. I just want to borrow them for a while."

"I'll keep your secret for now, but you have to return them."

"You've all done a great job distinguishing this area. Your town is picturesque and enchanting. But even if it weren't all that, you alone in the town would create that."

"I didn't know you were a poet! I could illustrate your poems, you know."

She was teasing him. They were having fun, and it'd been so long since he'd had fun with a woman, he didn't want to ruin it. But it was time.

"Piper..." A coal flamed in his throat. He doused it with a swallow. "Piper, I need...I'd like to tell you about Amy," he finished in a scratchy voice.

She put one hand on his back and rubbed her palm in small circles. The comforting gesture and her curious but nonjudgmental glance strengthened his courage.

He stationed one foot on the boulder and his elbow against his raised knee.

"We met in college, at the U-Dub, when I started my sophomore year. She was a freshman. I lived with my parents in Shoreline, near Seattle, where I grew up. Worked on campus at the newspaper. She had her own apartment near the U—her parents had a lot of money, and they paid for it. She wasn't a Christian, but by that time, I'd pretty much stopped going to church with my parents, unless it was a special occasion. They raised me right, but I thought I knew more than they did. It broke their hearts."

He closed his eyes, expecting the memories to sour his insides. But the delicate hand swirling circles on his back—was she drawing on it?—created a sweet impression instead.

"We...we found out we were pregnant as I was finishing up my junior year and just starting Appstract with a classmate." He hung his head, and the hand stilled, but only for a heartbeat before the soothing tracing coaxed the rest of the story from his vocal cords.

"We married immediately, but not because our parents forced us to. In fact, my parents advised me not to. They said just because a baby was on the way didn't mean we had to get married if we weren't right for each other. But we were in love, and I thought I knew better. I was going to be a dad. We had so much going for us. I'd graduate in a year, and I already owned my own startup."

"You don't have to finish if you don't want to," said the voice that belonged to the soothing hand. "I can guess the rest from here."

She was trying to spare him. But she needed to hear it all.

"We bought a small house in Shoreline. I'd created a traffic app that launched my career and the company. We showed my parents how wrong they were. Amy dropped out of college to have Jake. I thought we were living the dream. We fought a lot, but I figured we'd outgrow it. Mom and Dad kept inviting us to church, and I think we went the first Easter we were married, but that was it. Amy hadn't grown up in church. She believed in God, but she said the concept of Jesus was just too far out there for her."

Piper's fingers lightly massaged his rigid upper back through his sweatshirt. Her touch unwound the loops that had bunched tight.

"After Jake was born, she changed. She was never the same. She'd always been an emotional tightrope, but then she started calling me every couple of hours, wondering what I was doing and who I was with. I was a senior, and my partner and I had just moved our office to Belltown, so I was either at the university or at Appstract. But she never believed me. Made accusations. None of them were true."

Piper deserved better than him. As he heard his own words, he wondered how he could ever imagine she'd want a relationship with him.

But yet…a single finger treated his back like a canvas. He wondered what images this illustrator could possibly envision from his life with Amy.

He closed his eyes, but all he could summon up in his mind was the cute redhead beside him.

"She never let Jake out of her sight. Ever. But she didn't take him anywhere either. Please don't misunderstand. She was a good mom. She fed him healthy, played with him. But she wouldn't consider a babysitter. We never went out. I did all the shopping. My parents came to visit us a few times, but

Amy hovered over Jake and wouldn't allow Mom or Dad to even take him outside for a walk without her. I realize now she probably suffered postpartum depression after Jake was born, but I was young and didn't understand. I was rising up in Seattle's startup scene. Trying to deal with her constant texts and being a dad. I knew something was wrong, but not what. Until my mom sat me down. Told me she thought Amy needed help, and so did I."

He had to ask. "What is it that you're sketching on my back? I don't mind you using it as a drawing pad. I rather like it."

Her movement halted. "It's a verse, one of my favorites. Psalm 62:8: 'Trust in him at all times; ye people, pour out your heart before him. God is a refuge for us." As she spoke, her fingertips traced out the words between his shoulder blades. "You're talking to me, but I feel like you're pouring your heart out to God too."

He could never deserve someone like her. And yet...

"After that visit with my mom, Amy fell ill with an infection that affected her nervous system. Everything went haywire. Her heart wouldn't beat right. She couldn't breathe. For the first time in years, I found myself praying. Making all kinds of promises to God I could probably never keep. But He didn't spare her, and after a few days in the hospital, she was... she was gone."

Piper laid her head on his back but continued her tender rendering of the Bible verse on his bicep.

"Jake was two and half, and he went nuts when I tried to return to work without him, heaving and making himself sick. Mom came to stay with him for a few days until I could get him into daycare—but that never happened. And you pretty much know the rest. I told his pediatrician about this a few months ago. He said it's severe separation anxiety.

"Until we met you and Libby, I've only had a few minutes without him glued to me, when he goes to bed or naps. And even then I have to be there when he wakes up. I had to move his bed into my room at our condo. My parents did the same when I agreed to bring him to their cabin for the first time this winter. I was kind of like Libby. I didn't feel much like celebrating, but there's no way I couldn't celebrate Jesus's birth with my son..."

He inhaled the valley air, so different from the salty tang in Seattle. And more pure too. "I hardly remember her funeral, I was in such a grief daze. But my parents' preacher, Pastor Davis, said something that struck me—that God never leaves us or forsakes us. I'd forsaken Him, but He'd never left me. While Amy was sick, I turned to Him daily. And afterward too. Pastor Davis met with me and Jake for months, leading us every couple of weeks in prayer and Bible study. I started going back to church just two months before coming here."

She lifted her head off his back.

He turned so she could see his eyes, his sincerity. "I have a long way to go spiritually. We haven't known each other long either, and I don't know the future..." His thoughts picked up from where his voice had trailed off. *But I know if we have one I want to do it right this time.* How could he tell her that if he didn't know how it would go with Jake?

He wanted to kiss her until tomorrow, for the tenderness in her gaze.

Instead he kept his lips a safe distance from hers.

Chapter 13

Did the man who smiled every time he saw her, who let his son ride on the ATV with her sister, who would spend hundreds, if not thousands, on her Christmas event, who had endured hard times and still faced an uphill battle with Jake, hope he might have a future with her? A woman struggling to keep her sister on the straight and narrow and the alpaca farm from going under?

Was she reading too much into what he'd said?

She searched over her shoulder for the kids. Libby hoisted Jake off the ATV, near the maternity paddock. Piper doubted Sophia could resist Jake any more than the rest of them.

She reassigned her gaze to Alex, not doubting his sincerity, just the possibility of a future. That becoming-more-familiar melody struck a new, drawn-out chord, one of yearning.

But caution tempered her words.

"I don't know the future either, Alex."

He slid her one hand from his back and picked up her other so he held both of hers.

"Or even if we have one."

His Adam's apple bobbed as he swallowed audibly.

"I'm sorry for everything you've been through, but I'm so glad to hear you're mending your relationship with God. I have my own mending to do. I've even started praying with Libby

other than mealtimes. Well, this morning for the first time, bu
I'm going to try for every day. I've just been so…it's so harc
on Libby with Mom gone, and…and…" She let go of his hands
and slid off the boulder, listening to the trickle of the gentl
creek, glancing at the snow-flocked mountain barely visibl
now through the dusting of clouds. But her troubles didn'
diminish at the beauty of sight and sound.

She'd be as honest with him as he'd been with her.

"And…I don't know."

His arms wrapped around her middle, and his chin landec
on top of her head.

"My mom might not come back. I might have to finis
raising Libby on my own. And I'm doing a lousy job. I'm no
enough. She needs a mom. She deserves better. But this i
what we have. And I can't even consider leaving Cranberr
Creek or the ranch." She closed her eyes and leaned back in hi
arms. But the feeling of security was false. She couldn't lean o
him, on his strength. She couldn't expect him to add her anc
Libby to his troubled mix. To leave the city he obviously loved

His lips rested for a full five seconds against her head
"Piper, you're fantastic with her. I know you don't think so
and I can see she frustrates you to no end, but Callie was right
That girl is blessed to have you for a sister. And she's special
The way she is with Jake gives me hope for my future."

She gripped his arms to move them away from her, but h
only enfolded her hands into his and held her tighter.

"My dad's parents died before I was born, and my mom'
parents live abroad most of the time. Grandpa owns an import
export business. My aunts and uncles are all over the US. I
really is just Libby and me."

Enough. The more they spoke, the less chance it seemec

any long-term romance could develop between them. And Piper couldn't do short term with him. Yet here she stood in the circle of his arms.

"But none of these things are the real reasons it can't work between us."

His muscles tensed against her back. But they couldn't escape this essential truth.

"You're an iPhone guy. I'm a Samsung gal. You graduated from the U-Dub. I graduated from WSU. This side of the Cascades is Cougar country. And Huskies, well, around here, it's no Dawgs allowed. It's never going to work."

His hands slid under her sweatshirt and tickled her ribs through her henley. "This Husky would face down a Cougar any day!"

She wiggled out of his grasp, and he took off running toward the paddock. So much for facing her down! More like a Dawg with its tail tucked between its legs. Alex had no clue she ran thirty miles a week or that she'd run track in college. In half a second, she caught up to him and launched herself onto his back. He staggered but caught her legs.

"Even with a Cougar on his back, this Dawg's still standing. How in the world did you catch up to me anyway? My legs are way longer than yours."

"I'm an avid runn—"

"Dad, Dad!"

Alex chucked her off his back and dashed forward before skidding to halt. Close on his heels, Piper's momentum propelled her into him. He stumbled to the ground, and she landed on top of him, just as Libby drove up on the ATV.

Of course.

"Dad, Dad." Jake waved frantically.

He hadn't cried out in panic but to get Alex's attention.

"Wibby says it's time to go get a tree. She said we can help decorate it. She's going to wet me make an orny...orna..."

"Ornament." Libby lifted him off the ATV. "Jake helped me fill all the water bowls, and then we checked on Sophia. I really do think she's close, Piper.

"And hey, what are you two doing on the ground? Turn my back for a second..."

"Oh, stuff it, Libby. He ran toward Jake when he hollered Alex's name, and I banged smack dab into him." Piper scrambled to her feet as Alex sat up.

Libby stretched her arm toward Alex. "Need a hand, big brother?"

Jake walked behind his dad and started pushing on his upper back.

"I'm a big boy. I can manage." But he took Libby's hand anyway, and she tugged him up while Jake kept pushing from behind.

That girl! Giving me a hard time all night and all morning about that tree, about not decorating, but Jake steps on the property, and she acts like she was the one who insisted on a tree.

And what had Libby been thinking! *Big brother?* Did Alex even notice? And despite his hinting about a future together he hadn't whispered a word about not returning to Seattle permanently, and...could Piper risk continuing any sort of relationship with him? Could she manage Libby's drama, the ranch, illustrating, and her own broken heart on top of that?

"We're going to have to get all the stuff together to make Christmas cards for the kids too, Jake," Libby said as she settled Alex's son back on the ATV seat. "We'll let these two slowpokes walk back, and we'll go find the handsaw for your dad. You think he's strong enough to cut a tree down? Or will Piper and you have to do it?" She tossed Alex a devilish gleam as she revved the ATV.

"Hey!" Alex shouted as Libby spun out toward home. "I brought my dad's chainsaw, little sister!"

So he had noticed...

He slanted a fake grimace at Piper. "Can you believe her? Like I'll even let you touch that chainsaw. Ha!"

Piper sidled up to him and curled her fingers around his. She and Brisco set a meandering pace as her mind trailed off to something Libby had said to Jake moments ago.

Cards for the kids? Her sister and Jake had apparently brainstormed while riding around. That tenderhearted boy soothed Libby's heart, a balm on the wound left by their mother. Libby would miss that kid like crazy when Alex took Jake and headed for home. The snow-capped Cascade mountain range separated Piper's and Alex's hearts just as much as it divided Washington.

A divider that maybe neither could summit, not with the weight they carried on their backs.

But she supposed she should at least straighten this Seattleite out about the chainsaw.

"Umm, Alex, you know you don't usually cut down a Christmas tree with a chainsaw, right? Only a west-sider would think that."

"I knew that." His harrumph indicated the opposite.

He had obviously not talked to his father about why he needed to borrow the power tool.

"Not to worry. My dad kept a few handsaws in the shed. I know what I'm doing."

He sighed and rolled his eyes at the cloudy expanse above him, as if *she* didn't have a clue.

"You will not be handling the chainsaw or handsaw. That will be my job." He snickered. "You can haul it back to the truck."

"Did you bring a tarp?"

His blank expression said no.

"Don't worry. I have one of those too. That's what you use to haul out the tree."

"You just think you're so smart."

"I'm east-side smart!"

He dropped her hand and marched backward, facing her "These arms were built for Christmas tree cutting. And for carrying lovely ladies. And I can prove it. Hop back on. I'll give you a piggyback ride back to the house." He turned and held his arms out at his sides.

Piper surveyed the pasture and quarter-mile flat terrain to her home.

"No way!"

"Way!"

She deposited her hands on his shoulders and jumped up He captured her with an ease that had her rethinking the obstacles between them.

Maybe they wouldn't have to summit the mountain separately. Maybe God was strong enough to carry them both

Jake tugged on Alex's arm for the umpteenth time as they trudged up a hill at his dad's friend's property just off Highway 410, near Cliffdell, the same place they'd found Piper's nine- and ten-foot grand firs yesterday. Alex's mom thought she

should have a fresh-cut tree too, so he'd picked up another tree-cutting pass from the forest service office in Naches. But she wanted a noble with random branches. *Just ask for the impossible, Mom. Those are hybrids grown on tree farms.* Alex had looked it up on the internet.

Dad had intended to join them, but he'd been called out to resolve a snag in the house his construction company was building.

Alex scanned the proud but bare tamaracks and the evergreens in the heavily wooded mountainous region near the Wenatchee National Forest, something else he'd checked out on Google. How had he missed this his whole life? Sure, as a kid his parents had occasionally taken him tent camping to Camano Island State Park and near Deception Pass on Whidbey Island, but these picturesque woods, and the cabins and homes nestled among them, presented a nature-centered way of life. He and Jake needed to get out more, explore this side of the state. Not to mention, the plows and snowmobiles parked in driveways. Surely they indicated snow on the near horizon. His son had spouted off nonstop with glee at the overcast sky this morning.

Jake tugged his arm.

"No, I will not call Piper again." Nonetheless, Alex set down the chainsaw—since neither smarty-pants girl was here to object, he'd be using a power tool today—and scouted his sweatshirt pocket for his iPhone. He thumbed the button. Bummer. No service. He couldn't call her right now even if he wanted to. Which he did.

"Not that, Dad. I bin thinkin'."

Uh-oh.

His son fiddled with the play hammer in the loop in his new overalls. He insisted on wearing only work pants now, and flannels over his Transformer T-shirts. He wanted to be ready to help after Sophia's crias made their appearance.

"I really want to see the bats in Boulder Cave. We have a flashlight in the truck."

Alex gently pushed Jake to walk on ahead of him. "It's a little farther up from here, and Piper said the cave is closed for the winter. The bats don't like to be disturbed."

"But, Dad..."

Libby had gone on about the pitch-black Boulder Cave, the steep trail with massive cliffs that led to its entrance, and the fifty big-eared bats that wintered there. She'd said she'd be driving by summer—had ignored Piper's huff and shaking head—and that she'd take Jake there when the cave opened. As if Jake would still be hanging around Cranberry Creek in six months. As if Jake would go with her by himself.

The possibility of Jake driving off with Libby while Alex took a dressed-up Piper out on a real date, just the two of them, maybe to the new Yakima Steak Company she'd mentioned a couple times... Dare he even think such thoughts? Still, his mind painted an abstract watercolor of the two of them smiling at each other under shimmering lights. The few times his thoughts had flowed to a date with Piper, they'd always been on this side of the Cascades.

He understood she couldn't leave. He also wondered how he could even think of saying goodbye to her, to this region. His return to Seattle loomed closer every day.

Besides, he already owned a four-wheel-drive pickup perfect for this side of the state. He'd considered getting rid of the Dakota, as he didn't need two vehicles anymore. But he'd hang on to it now.

"Wook, Dad." Jake pointed to a scraggly noble. "What about this one?"

"That might work. But let's keep looking. Let's try for one taller, with less space between the branches."

"I bin thinkin' again."

"I can't call Piper, Jake. I told you. My phone doesn't have service. And Boulder Cave is closed."

"I know. But I don't wanna go to Wibby's after the crias are borned—"

"Born."

"Born."

"You don't?" Alex stumbled over a rock and almost dropped the chainsaw. Jake didn't want to go see the crias?

"I want to be there when they're borned. Born."

Alex imagined the string of questions that would spin out of Jake's mouth at that sight, like one of Piper's balls of yarn rolling along an endless wood floor. He didn't think he was ready to explain that much about the birds and the bees to his almost-four-year-old son.

Jake took off in a dead run ahead of him, temporarily abandoning the notion in light of a new discovery. But he would revisit it, that much Alex knew. Probably all the way back to the cabin. This conversation was far from over.

"This one, Dad. This one." Jake jumped up and down with one palm against a seven-foot noble, its branches fairly random, not too full, not to narrow.

Mom would love this one. Alex lifted the chainsaw, set it on choke, and pulled the cord once. He switched it to run and yanked the cord twice. And...nothing. It had started yesterday when his dad walked him through using it. He stared at it. Had he mixed up his dad's instructions?

"Try it again, Dad." Jake bounced around as if the ground were a trampoline.

"Jake, hold still." What was wrong with it? He set it on choke again and repeated the process, surprised when it fired up.

"Stand behind me, Jake, and don't move." Alex waited till Jake did as he said. He toppled the noble and flipped the kill switch on the chainsaw.

Why did he feel like a victor for cutting down a Christmas tree, as if he'd accomplished something major? Maybe the mountain air? He'd felt it yesterday too as he and Jake dragged Piper and Libby's trees down the hill. He could get used to this feeling. It compared to the natural high he experienced after a million downloads of an app he'd designed. If only that would happen with the ones users paid for and not just the free ones. he'd be a millionaire by now.

"Wet's haul it to the truck, Dad! Grandma will be so happy."

A contentment he hadn't felt in years, maybe never arranged a harmony of hope in Alex's heart. Hope for the future. For him and Jake. Maybe him and Piper and Jake and Libby? And the best way he could think to celebrate that was right here, with his son, in the same manner as Piper had done with Libby.

"Come here, Jake," Alex said as he sank to his knees and pulled Jake onto his lap.

"What, Dad? Why are we sitting here?"

"I thought...I thought we'd take a moment and pray together."

"Wike with Pastor Davis?"

"Yeah, like that. But with just me and you."

"Wike before we eat?" he asked, one eyebrow raising as the other dipped.

Right then Alex committed to praying at least once a day with Jake when a meal wasn't involved. Granted, that'd be hard, considering Jake's voracious appetite. But if Piper could strive for that with Libby, he could certainly do the same with Jake. They'd begin now. And maybe when Jake crawled into bed tonight too.

"Can I pray, Daddy?"

Alex had imagined himself praying, but he'd go with the flow.

"Sure, buddy." He twined his fingers around Jake's folded hands.

"Thank you, Jesus, for Dad and Papa and Grandma. Bless Wibby and Piper. And Sophia and her crias. Help them to be borned...born today. And please remember that I haven't ever seen a snowflake. Amen."

"In Jesus's name I pray. Amen," Alex said softly.

"In Jesus's name I pray. Amen."

Jake shot to his feet. "Will God make it snow now? Can I go watch the crias being borned...born?"

Chapter 14

Libby paced around the barn, fingers fluttering, her anxiety churning a dented ring in the straw on the cement floor. No matter how many times Emi and Piper insisted that Sophia needed calm vibes and that she could sense anxiety, Libby's swirling emotions transferred to her hands and feet. Whenever she stopped pacing, her foot tapped a staccato beat or her fingers drummed a rhythm on a railing.

When Libby's next rotation passed her in front Emi, the vet snatched Libby's arm and plonked her onto a bale of hay. "Sit, chica. You're making *me* nervous, and Emerita Silva never panics." Her hands kneaded Libby's shoulders. "Sophia delivered a cria just fine last year. I'm probably not even needed here for her. You, however, need the expert touch of my nimble hands." She flexed her fingers, settled a fist onto Libby's upper back, and pushed. "You're so uptight that I'm about ready to send you packing to the house. I'll text you when you can come out."

"Not a chance. I'm not leaving this barn. Not with Sophia in labor."

Piper sat next to her on the hay bale and rubbed her shoulder against Libby's. "Even if only one cria makes it, we'll never sell it. It'll be all yours forever. I promise."

"You know you shouldn't sell either of them for breeding anyway, chica. You shouldn't perpetuate twin births, as cool as this is. The mothers don't make enough milk for two usually. Mikko and Pikko will be wonderful companions and produce great fiber. But that's it."

Libby tapped the ball of her booted foot on the cement floor at a tempo even a Riverdance performer couldn't have matched.

"What if neither survives? We always talk like *one* will live for sure, but we don't know. Besides, I don't want just one for me. I want Jake to have one too. What will I tell him if... if...only Mikko survives. Mikko is supposed to be his. Pikko is supposed to be mine."

Though unspoken between them, if only one lived, it'd be named Mikko, in honor of Jake.

Libby's statement rippled a judder of unease through Piper's stomach. Her sister spoke as if Jake would be a permanent fixture in her life, as if Piper and Alex were a foregone conclusion, a period at the end of a declarative sentence. But in truth, their relationship was more of a question mark at the end of an interrogative sentence.

Emi must have sensed Piper tensing up, because she transferred her hands from Libby to Piper, and her magical fingers manipulated Piper's body into a semi-relaxed state.

Thank God, truly, Piper's childhood friend had decided to practice in the valley after graduating from veterinary school.

She was three years older than Piper, but they'd grown up in Sunday school and youth group at church, and when Callie had joined them as a teenager after being taken in by a Cranberry Creek foster family, it had been more *three's company* than *three's a crowd.*

Piper couldn't have conceived of Emi not being there for the births. And more importantly, for the emotional support for her and Libby.

Libby crossed her leg and jiggled her toe at a speed that blurred Piper's vision. She grabbed her sister's knitting project out of her bag.

She waved the yarn and needles in front of Libby's face. "Here, I knew you'd need something to keep you busy. Give Emi's hands a break. All you have left is a couple rows of decreases and the bind off. Finish up your hat for Jake before it snows."

The reddish-hued thickly clouded sky implied snow was as imminent as the crias' birth. Jake must be over the moon.

Sophia, on the other hand, like most alpaca mamas, would have preferred a bright, sunny day. The sun had poked through briefly this morning. It must have been enough for her.

Libby flicked the project from Piper's hand. "Okay, okay, I'm fine now." She held the hat in front of her face. "Darn it, a couple stitches dropped off. I knew I should have capped off these needles."

Emi shoved a bale up to the one occupied by Libby and Piper. "If that doesn't settle her down, she really is going to have to go in," Emi whispered as she lodged herself next to Piper.

"Hey, Emerita Silva, I'm right here. I can hear you, you know. I'll behave. I'll behave. I just have to bind off now, and this hat will be ready for Jake's cute little head."

"Good. Then you can get started on one for the event."

Libby sighed. "I do have a life, you know. Besides, Jake and I are going to be making cards for the kids. Jake's crazy about the idea of using glue. I'm going to show him some designs on the computer and let him pick out a few. Then we're going to print them up and glue on die cuts."

She held up the brown nubby hat for Piper's perusal. "Done! Do you think he'll like it? Really like it?"

Piper squished the cap around in her hands and then slightly stretched the baby cables. "He'll love it, Libby. I don't know how you make those cables look so real. And I love that little accent green row after the ribbing." She stashed it in the bag. "But since you can't make cards out here, why don't you start on anoth—"

The scraping of the barn door pushed Piper to her feet. Had Emi texted Callie, and she'd decided to join them? But who was manning Imagknitive? Callie's mom? Saturdays were always so busy there.

"Piper, Wibby, are you in here?"

Two little hands in work gloves appeared below the large masculine hands shoving the door open.

"My dad said you're prob'ly in the barn. Did Sophia have Mikko and Pikko yet? Daddy said I could watch!" Jake hugged Piper's legs.

"Jake, I told you, you have to be quiet," Alex said.

Jake conferred the same hug on Libby.

Piper had texted Alex about fifteen minutes ago that Sophia had gone into labor this morning. Alex hadn't hinted he'd show up with Jake. She hadn't even known he was back in Cranberry Creek after his flight to Seattle yesterday. She'd planned to just text him when it was all over, one way or the other.

Alex grinned and cupped her cheek with a gentle hand. Wait. Was that a callus she felt?

"Surprise. The big day, huh? I begged Jake to let me come and be here with you guys. I bugged him and whined all morning until he finally gave in and said we should fly back to Yakima early."

"Hey, you didn't ask me! I asked you. Get it right, Dad!" Jake plunked his hands on his hips. "Did you see the sky, Wibby? I prayed for snow. I prayed for snow when we were at our condo too. My dad told me God wistens when I pray."

"My sister told me the same thing. Let's watch Sophia right now, and then we'll watch the sky for a while."

Her eyes beamed a question at Alex.

Hesitation painted creases onto his forehead.

"He's a kid," Emi said as she walked up to Jake. "Hi, Jake. I'm Emi. I'm the doctor for the alpacas." She glanced at Alex. "Let him watch. It'll be good for him. We could see a nose poke out any second. And if I have to intervene, Jake can go snowflake gazing with Libby."

"But what if only one—"

"Don't say it, Piper." Libby hugged Jake tight against her legs. "Emi says Jake will be fine. No matter what, we'll both be fine. Can he watch, Alex? I've been watching crias be born my whole life. Look how good I turned out." She scrunched her nose and flashed an impish grin.

At Alex's nod, she moved Jake closer to Sophia's pen.

Alex hooked his left arm around Piper just as Emi marched up to them, her jet-black waist-length hair swinging out and then rippling down her back, a determined glint in her dark-brown eyes. Had she remembered him from when they were kids?

"I've heard so much about that boy of yours, Alex. He's a gem. I'm glad you brought him. All children should be exposed to farm life at some point in their lives." Emi grasped the hand Alex held out.

"Since his first visit, Jake has begged me every day to bring him here." Alex clamped Piper tighter to his side and dropped a kiss to her head.

"I bet he didn't have to try too hard to convince you." Emi's sparkling eyes and dry tone spoke volumes. "Does he have a pet of his own?"

Mmm, that question wasn't even subtle! *That's right, Emi. Just blindside the poor guy.* Piper needed new friends. Friends who knew how to behave around potential boyfriends. Friends who didn't boldly try to direct her relationship with a man—right in front of the guy!

"Uh, our condo doesn't allow pets. But since Jake's done so well with the alpacas and dogs here, my parents have talked about getting a dog that's good with kids. What breed would you recommend, Emi?"

Oh, Piper was so proud of him. He was good at deflecting.

And Emi took the bait.

"So many parents pick a Labrador retriever for their kids and they're great, but high strung and hard to train to walk on a leash. But if you want a dog that's more trainable, that Jake could actually—"

"Dad! Daddy! I see...I see a nose. And a...and...what is that Wibby?"

"Those are feet. Piper, Emi, Alex, it's happening. It's happening! Oh, I don't know if I can stand it." Libby picked up Jake and paced the trail she'd already blazed in front of the pen.

"Do you want me to take him, Libby?" Alex propped his hands on Jake's waist.

"No, no. It's just...it's just. Maybe he shouldn't watch Maybe I shouldn't watch."

"I'll be fine, Wibby. I just want to know how the twins got in there."

"Jake, I told you," Alex said. "No questions—"

"It's called *breeding*," Libby said overtop Alex. "Like your dad said, no more questions. Just watch."

Jake patted her arm, and Libby straggled to a stop, facing the stall. Alex positioned his right arm across Piper's shoulders, and Piper curved her arm around Libby's back.

"That mama's not having any trouble," Emi said after a few minutes. "I've examined her fully. There's nothing more I can do unless there's a glitch with the delivery. It's all up to her now."

Jake watched wide eyed, not uttering a word. Piper figured Libby's arms must be killing her. No way could she hold Jake for much longer. But no way would she put him down either, unless Jake or Alex insisted.

Alex cleared his throat. "I wonder...I wonder...would it be all right to pray?"

"My dad prays good. He even wets me pray."

"That's an even better idea, Jake, if it's okay with your dad," Piper said. "Libby and I would love it if you prayed."

Alex's quick nod signaled a sense of relief at Piper's initiative.

Libby lowered Jake to the ground.

He folded his hands. "Close your eyes, everyone.

"Dear Jesus, Callie says You made the animals. And that You do miracles. So please wet Mikko and Pikko be born safe. And remember, I've never seen a snowflake. Amen. In Jesus's name. Amen.

"Did I do it right?"

"You did it just perfect! Did Callie teach you that in Sunday school?" Libby pulled him against her.

"Yeah, she said Jesus does miracles. Maybe He'll do one today."

"You're a little prayer warrior. Thank you!" Libby turned him to the stall. "Look, Jake. The first one's about to drop."

"Will it hurt?"

"No, it's okay. It's...nature."

Piper dashed forward and placed a towel where the cria would drop in a few seconds, then retreated back to Alex.

Piper held her breath at the sight. She didn't really know how Alex was doing, standing in a barn, watching an alpaca deliver crias. Her and Libby's everyday life probably felt like an out-of-this-world experience to a guy who lived and worked in a swanky area in Seattle. But his sticking by her side when the outcome was still so uncertain balanced her unstable emotions. She'd fretted about Libby falling into a deep funk if these twins didn't survive. But his presence here stabilized Piper, made her feel as if she weren't alone.

As if Alex supported her.

He kept running his fingers through her hair. If they snagged in a tangle—and her curls tended to knot—he simply smoothed it out.

He spoke close to her ear. "I've never seen you with your hair down before. As cute as you look in a ponytail, I've never even thought about it. Jake really didn't have to beg me too hard this morning. I'd already booked us on an earlier flight because I couldn't get a certain redhead out of *my* head." He laughed. "It's a good thing I didn't see you with your hair down before we flew out. I might never have made it to the airport."

Several minutes later, Libby jumped up and down, swung

Jake around by the arms, hugged Piper and Alex, and started all over.

She grabbed Piper and danced a jig in a circle with her. "Oh, Piper. I just didn't think...I was so scared. But look at them! They're so beautiful."

Piper squeezed her tight. "It's a *Merry Christmas* to us from God."

Libby raised Jake up over her head and spun. "One for you and one for me!"

She set him on a bale of hay, and he hopped up and down, clapping. "Which one is Mikko and which one is Pikko?"

That brought Libby to an abrupt halt. Her head twisted from the crias to Jake.

"We'll sort out their names later."

Her exhilaration coated the air in the barn. Piper could almost inhale the girl's excitement.

Emi leaned over the pen. "A male and a female, I think, and they're beautiful. But I need to get them weighed and checked out. You all go in the house and have some goodies while I'm taking care of this. I think Libby made some Christmas cookies yesterday. I can confirm that they are heavenly. I'll text you if anything's amiss, Piper."

"Yeah, and Piper made an apple pie. Which she hardly ever does." Libby jerked her head Alex's direction. "And it doesn't take a genius to figure out why. She even baked it on the Traeger. It looks amazing."

Okay, so Piper had hoped to see Alex sometime today or tomorrow.

She tucked Libby's arm into hers as they headed out of the barn and toward the house, Libby's smile a beam of brightness in the late-afternoon cloudy air.

"A snowflake! Dad, I see a snowflake!"

Piper swung Libby around so they faced Jake and Alex. Jake stood there with his nose pointed toward the sky, his hands out and palms up.

"God did hear me. You're right, Dad. He wistens! It's snowing, just wike you promised, Wibby."

He twirled in a circle as snowflakes landed on his hair and nose, a light dusting already gluing to the frozen ground.

"We'll have to fire up that tractor, Jake," Libby said. "Once the ground is covered, we'll plow a figure eight in the pasture and line it with straw so the alpacas can graze that way. You will love that tractor!

"Oh, I forgot. Wait here!" She bolted toward the barn, her feet barely touching the ground.

"They're so soft on my cheeks, Daddy." Jake stretched his neck back as far as he could manage.

Piper braced him with her hand to keep him from toppling backward.

Alex crouched beside Jake and tipped his head back just like his son. "Maybe tomorrow or the next day we can sled down that hill by Papa and Grandma's. Or build a snowman. Or make a snow angel."

"A snow angel! With wings?"

Libby skidded to a stop beside Jake and knelt in front of him. She held up her handiwork. "I finished it, Jake. Just for you."

Jake relocated the stocking cap from her hand to his head. "Wow! My own cap. Can I wear it when we go snowboarding, Wibby?"

"Sure, Jake. I said I'd teach you." She folded Jake's hand into hers. "Let's go find a good spot to build a snowman. And maybe you and your dad can go to the implement parade in Sunnyside tonight. You'd love that."

"What's a imple...imple..."

"Implement."

"Implement parade?"

"We go when it's dark out, and the tractors and combines and antique cars are all decorated and lit up like Christmas trees. It's a famous parade. You'll love it..."

Their voices trailed off as Libby raced Jake to the chestnut tree. She didn't just let him win either. They touched at the same instant.

"What do you think about the parade tonight? It sounds like fun, if it's not a blizzard out," Alex asked.

"I have to stay and monitor the crias. I'm not going anywhere. But you should take Libby and Jake. He'll love it. Ask your parents to go along. It's a great parade. It's even been featured on the Travel Channel."

Alex slid his arms around Piper from behind. She gripped his forearms with her hands. A day that could have ended in disaster had instead turned into a complete blessing. She relaxed against his sturdy chest.

"Some wishes came true today," he said softly. "Libby's and Jake's prayers were answered."

"I don't know if you really know how amazing it is." Piper could hardly believe it herself. "They both survived. Cria twins just don't happen. I feel like maybe God set this whole birth in motion just for Libby, because He knew how much she'd need it right now. How much *I* needed it. I know they're just animals, but I feel like Jake nailed it. We witnessed a miracle. I just can't get over it."

"I can't get over you," Alex said as he rotated her.

Piper sucked in her breath as his lips grazed first one cheek and then the other. He kissed each eyebrow and her nose. Couldn't he find her lips? *This guy!* She fisted the hair at the nape of his neck and shifted his head to just the right spot. His lips lowered and lowered until finally, finally, they landed on hers, a featherlight touch that sparked a yearning deep inside.

A yearning for something more. For something that maybe he couldn't give her.

His lips proceeded to her forehead, and his fingers journeyed through her hair yet again.

"I can't wait to take you to Seattle with us," Alex said. "And I'm glad the kids are always around, I think."

He didn't add anything to that. He didn't need to. She knew what he meant. She was kind of glad the kids were always around too. Piper already loved Jake, and it was clear Alex cared for Libby. He'd probably spoil her as much as Mom did.

As for Seattle, that measure hadn't been played out yet. What if the final notes trilled when they crossed the Cascades, stepped on his turf, and viewed him and Jake in their true environment?

She wouldn't worry about that on a day like today. She had a couple of weeks to work herself up over the possibility that she and Libby might never see Jake and Alex again after New Year's, except when they visited his parents. And what if not even then?

Chapter 15

Alex held his elbow out, and Piper looped her arm through it.

"I can read your thoughts, you know," Alex said as they followed the footprints left by Libby and Jake.

He chuckled at the momentary alarm on her face. He didn't know how she could look so gorgeous after spending all morning in a barn, but her features radiated genuine happiness. A gloomy something had dimmed her eyes for just a moment, but as her lips curled up again and her eyes sparkled at him, he wondered if he'd imagined it.

"I've been working on my mind-reading ability ever since I met you." Alex chuckled. "You're wondering when Jake's birthday is, so I'll tell you. It's Monday. My parents are planning on taking us out. I know it's not like a real date or anything, but we'd love it if you and Libby joined us."

Alex wondered at the relief that etched her features. What had she really been thinking? He'd have to study her countenance more. Maybe he could design a mind-meld app that would estimate her thoughts based on her facial expressions. Yeah. She'd appreciate that, for sure.

She hugged his elbow close to her side.

"Libby and I would love that, if Callie or Emi can stay here for a couple of hours. Do you think...do you think someday we'll go on a real date, just me and you? Never mind. It's okay. Truly. I think Jake has made real headway. And Libby and Jake together, well, just look at them."

He believed her that it was okay. He had to. Because if it wasn't... But before he could genuinely consider anything long term with Piper, he had to resolve Jake's separation anxiety disorder and his own role in it. While in Seattle last time, he'd contacted a therapist Jake's pediatrician had recommended. And just in case, he'd called Children's Village too. The calls had surged hope through him.

But neither had produced the optimism that visibly presented itself every time he saw his son with Libby and Piper. Could they do more for Alex and Jake than any therapist? That was irrelevant. He'd never consider placing that kind of burden on either sister. But what if God's plan for restoration revolved around these two, and what if he and Jake were to help mend the ache left by Piper and Libby's disappearing mother?

Could it be? What if it all centered on God's grace and not their own plans and ideas? Their lives seemed so crazy. Could God really be that amazing, that what they saw as unpredictable and unsolvable, He viewed as an opportunity to extend His grace?

Alex's glance drifted toward his son and the pretty teen at the chestnut tree in the distance. Jake sat in the tire swing, legs sticking straight out and hands gripping the top, his face tipped back to welcome any snowflakes that drifted through the bare branches as Libby pushed the swing.

"They keep each other so occupied." Alex stopped Piper by the fence.

"They do! I can't get over how much Jake brings out the best side of Libby."

"And she reduces his panic level by visible degrees. She takes after her sister in the special department."

Maybe he really could read her mind and wouldn't need that app after all. Their thoughts certainly followed the same trajectory.

"We'll have a lot to do the next three weeks to get ready for the event. Callie arranged for the families to come the Saturday before Christmas. I hope Jake knows what he's let himself in for. You too. Libby plans to introduce Jake to a glue stick. Sorry that means you'll be spending so much time with us. I'm sure you're bummed about that. But you can work from the kitchen table just like I do."

She angled her head to the side so that he could see her mischievous look.

"I for one am happy to stick to you like glue," he said.

"That's a cliché! You can do better than that."

"Sorry. You're the creative one."

He straightened and scanned the yard through the powdery snowfall. "Where's Libby and Jake?"

Piper rushed toward the tree. That girl could book it, even in the snow! He really did need to hit the gym more. And buy his own work boots. She wasn't even out of breath when she reached the tire swing. He tried to control his panting as he supported the tree with his backside. This ancient thing might topple at any moment.

Neither kid waited in the yard, but no cries of *Dad, Dad* reverberated through the snow-thickened air either.

Piper aimed a finger toward the avenue of footprints that led to the back deck. She stepped forward as if to follow the path, but he grasped her arm.

He might not be able to read Piper's mind, but God surely

read Alex's every thought and heard his every prayer, even the unspoken ones of his heart.

Piper leaned her back against the tree, the dawning of realization replacing the apprehension on her face.

"Alex."

Her soprano whisper drifted over his ears lighter than the flakes trickling through the branches. He knew the words that would flow from her mouth as surely as he knew his lungs would eventually inhale again.

Maybe. If he didn't die from shock first.

"Alex," she whispered again, her face turned toward the house.

That beautiful farmhouse. Where his son probably sat at the table—or, knowing Libby, in the family room on the sectional—eating Alex's share of cookies and apple pie. Without Alex. Without panicking?

Do you think we'll watch another miracle today?

"Do you think we'll see another miracle today?"

He'd been pretty close.

If he spoke, that meant he still breathed, right?

"Let's just wait here for a few minutes." He wheezed, like the sound of an espresso machine pressing out steamed milk. "I think God's trying to kill me with this miracle. I can't catch my breath."

He curved forward, his palms against his knees. "Just when I was making all these plans in my head for how to fix me and Jake..." He simply couldn't spit out another word.

A delicate hand rubbed his arm, and then she lightly pressed her upper body and head against his back for too brief a minute.

He aligned with the tree again when she lifted away. He

thrust his body away from the trunk and curled his fingers around her hands.

"You know what I want to do right now more than anything?"

"Kiss me? While no one's watching? Or would that be too weird?"

"Besides that. We're safer if someone's watching."

"Agreed."

"I want to pray with you. Will you pray with me, Piper?"

Without hesitation, she nodded and bowed her head.

Alex echoed her movements but found for a moment he didn't know what to pray.

"Dear Father, we don't even know what's going to happen next, but You know. And that's enough. May Your grace be enough for us." He peeked at Piper when she squeezed his fingers, and saw her nodding. Could he finish his prayer with his eyes open? "And thank You for the precious gifts, the miracle of the twin crias. For Jake stepping out of his comfort zone. Thanks for never leaving us, even when we forget You."

"And thank You so much for the friendship between Libby and Jake, Lord," Piper interjected. She presented wide eyes to Alex and whispered, "Is it okay if I pray too?"

Okay? It was great. "Of course."

She scrunched her eyes closed. "Help us to cast all our cares on You."

He linked his fingers with hers. "Let's be brave."

Together they made their way onto the back deck and through the entry to the dining room, expecting to hear the pitter-patter of Jake's feet as soon as the door clicked shut. His son's work boots sat next to Libby's larger pair by the door, one tipped over on its side.

Nothing. No feet rushed his direction. Alex paused at the peninsula in the kitchen as he overheard voices in the great room. Piper tiptoed up beside him. He stretched across the counter, leaning on his elbows.

Libby sat on the sofa with Jake, a tablet propped on her lap but sloped his way. Jake held a half-eaten snowman Christmas cookie in each hand.

"What do you think about that card, Jake?"

"Well, there's no Bumble Bee on it either."

"Do they all have to have a Transformer on them?"

Oh, welcome to Alex's world!

"Can't some of them have Spider-Man, and maybe a dinosaur, and a few Hello Kitty cards too?"

"Actually, girls wike Transformers too. My grandma plays with them."

Alex and Piper erupted in laughter, and the children's heads jerked their way.

"Oh, hi, Dad. Hi, Piper."

"Oh, hi, Dad?" That's it? After a year and a half? Jake didn't jump off the love seat. Didn't cry out. Didn't insist Alex come into the room.

He didn't even keep looking at his dad. He tilted his head back to the tablet.

"Maybe one card with Spider-Man and one with a brontosaurus and one with Hello Kitty. But that's it."

A finger penned calligraphy onto Alex's upper back.

"Another verse?" He twisted just enough on his elbow so he could see her expression.

An elfin gleam glowed from her eyes.

"No. More like, 'Welcome to *The Twilight Zone*.'"

Chapter 16

Piper tossed a third pair of black slacks onto the Irish-chain quilt—one her mother had sewn, in shades of plum and white—on her white panel bed. She'd never fretted even once about what to wear to Seattle any of the numerous times she'd been there before. But when a girl had to compete with the glorious views of the Emerald City for the attention of the guy of her dreams, she needed all the help she could get. Didn't she have a single pair of black pants that flattered her?

If only her legs were as long as Libby's!

Which reminded her. If she didn't hustle her sister along, they wouldn't be ready when Alex and Jake picked them up at ten this morning. Only a half hour from now. She spread her arms across the doorframe and leaned into the hall.

"Libby, baby, you better be packed and ready when they get here."

"Get a grip, Piper."

Libby's voice came from downstairs rather than her room across the hallway. Why wasn't she in her bedroom getting ready?

"You made me pack last night, remember? I'm waiting for you! Do you need help up there?"

"You goin' to come up and help me? Really?"

"NAC, big sister."

Piper really needed a teen-lingo dictionary.

But Libby was on it. "Means *not a chance.* I'll send Emi and Callie up though."

They'd arrived late last night, Callie to farm sit and Emi to stand by. Piper and Emi had introduced Callie to Mikko and Pikko. The tenderhearted Callie, to no one's surprise, had volunteered to spend the night in the barn with them, saying she'd bonded with the twins. But Piper and Emi had dragged her by her hands across the snow-covered ground, out the gate, and past the snowmen Libby and Jake had built in the front yard while Piper and Alex enjoyed mint mochas and conversation in the house.

They'd pacified Callie by playing her favorite card game, and later they'd dozed off on the sectional and recliner in the family room so they could sleep under the glow of the nine-foot Christmas tree Libby had taken charge of decorating. But mostly they'd talked nonstop until 5:00 a.m. Which explained why Piper couldn't get her act together this morning.

She shook out another pair of black slacks. Skinnier. A bit stretchier. She'd last worn them to Kiddles, before leaving Spokane. These would work. She shimmied into them and slid her arms into an emerald scooped-neck sweater with an asymmetrical hem, a gift from Callie last Christmas.

She slipped her feet into high-heeled black ankle boots. With her luck, she'd probably slip in the snow, break an ankle, and miss the trip.

She swished her curls around with her fingers. She'd worn her classic ponytail all week, but today she'd wear it down. Maybe it'd give her a competitive edge.

But if the sun shone in Seattle today, she was sure that would spell her doom.

Emi and Callie trooped into the room and threw themselves across Piper's bed.

"Wow, it's a mess in here," Callie said. "Hey, you're wearing the sweater I made. Look out, Seattle!"

"What's Libby wearing? Not that Mickey Mouse sweatshirt, right?" Piper asked Callie.

"Oh yeah. Her skinniest, most torn-looking jeans, UGGs, and Mickey Mouse."

Piper sighed. If she made her change, Libby would pitch a fit, and she didn't have time for that.

"Emi, why are you still here?" Piper asked.

"I just got back from a call. Poor calf with scours—"

"We don't need the details. TMI." Piper unzipped her carry-on overnight case and added a pair of glittery silver strappy sandals, just in case she ended up wearing the black dress she'd managed to wedge in.

"Is there anything I need to get in Seattle for the Kids and Crias day?" she asked Callie.

"You crazy, girl?" Callie said, kicking her heels back and forth against her bottom. "You four have been a whirlwind the last couple weeks. Your yard looks like a zoo of lights. Alex even strung icicles around the barn! He's a keeper—I'm tellin' ya, Piper."

She agreed. If only Seattle would let him go. Or maybe if he'd let Seattle go. And if the kids would cooperate.

"Grant, his dad, helped. And yeah, they did great."

"And, chica, I love the big ornaments you added to the dogwoods and blue spruce. And the tree in the barn—spectacular!"

Where had Piper put her red purse? She hardly ever switched out purses. Too much of a nuisance. She started opening the drawers in her dresser.

"We're expecting about twenty kids." Callie continued as if Emi hadn't even spoken.

It was hard to get a word in edgewise with Callie. Good thing Emi was used to it.

"Jake and Libby made forty cards, so you're covered. We already have thirty hats for the kids, and I've asked several women to work up a few headbands for the foster moms. Alex arranged Smokin' Joe's Barbecue to cater lunch. And best of all, you'll get to show off the twin crias some more. And that article in the newspaper a couple days ago was great. You even got a mention, Emi."

"Mikko and Pikko are *famoso* worldwide, superstars in the alpaca industry. The Associated Press picked up the article and I've received calls from several vets in the US and about four different countries."

Emi, whose grandparents had emigrated from Mexico in the 1960s, didn't speak a lick of Spanish. She just tossed a few words in for good measure. *Probably in the wrong order.*

"What are you looking for, chica?"

"My red purse! It's not in my closet. It's not in my dresser." She slammed the bottom drawer shut with her foot.

"You're in a tizzy, girl. Settle down." Emi rolled onto her back, swinging Piper's handbag from one finger. "You mean the one I've been lying on?"

Piper swiped the purse from Emi and plunked down on the edge of her bed. She. Would. Not. Cry. She hated tears. Red swollen eyes. Massive headaches. Exhaustion. Red swollen eyes. Had she said that already?

Callie immediately propped herself up beside Piper, her intuitive violet eyes squinting.

Uh-oh. I should have pulled myself together before they came into my bedroom. Why didn't we do this last night, when we had time? She checked her phone. Five minutes. If Alex wasn't early. *Please don't be early.*

"What are you so afraid of? Isn't Jake a lot better?"

Piper flung herself backward. "Yes, as long as Jake knows Alex is nearby, he'll help Libby with chores, go to the barn with her, even go for short walks with me or his grandparents. And Alex said Jake moved into his own room at the cabin. That's a big deal. But we haven't tried a date yet. We don't want to push our luck."

After Jake's birthday party at Firehouse Pizza Parlor, a restored historic firehouse, Alex had invited Piper and Libby out to his parents' beautiful cedar home—hardly the cabin Alex kept calling it. The four adults had spent part of the evening marveling at the change in Jake.

"What then? Libby?"

Piper shook her head against her silk and cotton plum comforter. "She's been way better! Every minute she doesn't spend with Jake, and most minutes she does, she's out in the barn or paddocks with those crias. I know she still misses Mom, and she didn't even want to exchange presents. Until Jake asked her what she wanted for Christmas. Now suddenly she and I are exchanging one gift. Yesterday was her last day of school. She promised to teach Jake to snowboard, so I'll probably have to head up the mountain a couple times a week. She's not going on the weekends though. I'm so not standing in those long lines to get on the lifts."

Callie drummed her fingers on Piper's knee.

"Alex," Emi said.

"So it all comes down to Alex," Callie said at the same time.

Piper rolled to her side and propped herself up on her elbow. "No."

"If not Alex, then who, chica?"

"Hey, that's my signature, Callie." Emi socked Callie's arm. "Come up with your own."

"All right, all right."

"If not Alex, then who, chica?" Emi turned a menacing squint in Callie's direction.

"Her," Callie said.

"Her who?"

"Her *Piper*." Callie tapped Piper's head.

Piper struggled to believe that a great guy like Alex would give up what must be a huge part of his life, the city where he'd grown up, gone to college, married his wife, had an office and a partner and staff...for her. For her and Libby, really. And was it right for her to want him to? Especially since she wasn't willing to make the same sacrifice for him?

He'd been so great these last two weeks, but she'd pulled back. The thought of his leaving hurt too much.

"Hey, Piper, get your butt down here. Our ride's here."

Libby's voice vaulted Piper off the bed. She tossed her black leather jacket—plenty warm for Seattle weather—over one arm and picked up her carry-on.

"Just when we're getting to the good stuff!" Callie muttered "Put your coat on. It's not snowing, but it's freezing out."

"Yes, Mommy," Piper said.

"And don't worry," Emi said from the bed. "Like good friends, Callie and I will figure out what's wrong with you and call you with instructions for dealing with yourself. After we sleep on it, of course."

"You girls just make sure that the twin crias—all the alpacas—are healthy when I get home tomorrow. I'll figure myself out, thank you very much."

Not likely, given the mountain standing between her and her guy.

"I want Wibby to buckle me in." Jake swatted Alex's hands away.

"I told you not to get unbuckled, Jake," Alex said. "The girls are coming out." Jake could unbuckle now, but he couldn't clip everything back into place.

"But I want to go see Mikko and Pikko! Why couldn't I wear my work jeans today?"

"You didn't wear them when we flew to Seattle last week either. We have a business meeting, Jake. These are your office jeans. And I told you. We have to be at the airport at eleven to catch the noon flight out of Yakima. You can see the crias tomorrow."

He dropped the tailgate and rolled back the tonneau cover on the pickup bed. The colored lights on the bushes and trees reflected off the snow on this gray nondrizzly day. Piper had let him and his dad go all out with the lights, wanting to make the ranch as cheerful and Christmasy for her event as possible. Libby and Jake had taken charge of building and outfitting snowmen. They'd constructed four, approximately the heights of Piper, Alex, Libby, and Jake. Jake's idea, Libby had said, but Alex wasn't so sure. That girl lacked any sort of subtlety. Which Alex found refreshing.

This would be his and Jake's fifth flight to Seattle since arriving in Cranberry Creek, and the first time Jake had fussed. Alex could have driven. It was only a little more than a three-hour road trip. But he preferred to fly over Snoqualmie Pass than drive over it any more than he had to, considering delays because of snow or ice or avalanche control.

Jake didn't see why they had to go to the office anymore now that Mikko and Pikko had been born. He preferred the barn to Belltown.

"That's all the luggage you girls have?" Alex asked when he saw Piper's and Libby's small suitcase carry-ons. "When my mom comes, even for a short visit, she packs a huge suitcase."

"We're fine, Alex," Libby said as Alex lifted her pink leopard-print case into the back of the pickup.

Egad. She sounded just like Jake. He was rubbing off on her.

He lifted Piper's plum-colored carry-on but then set it down on the tailgate, one hand still gripping the handle. She looked stunning in her green sweater and black slacks and boots, her red curls draping nearly to her elbows. As beautiful as she looked, her eyes interested him the most. A glint of trepidation shimmered from those chocolatey depths. He'd like to kiss all her fears away.

And maybe soon he'd do just that.

Was she nervous about flying over the Cascades? She'd mentioned she'd only driven to the west side before.

"Piper, if you'd rather not—"

"Stop staring at Piper," Libby said as she slammed her door. "You've seen her every day this week. And she's just all nervous about going to Seattle with you. Like she's in some big competition with the city or something."

"Libby!" Piper exclaimed. "She's just making stuff up to be irritating."

Alex hugged her with one arm while closing the tailgate with the other, briefly flicking his fingers through her hair.

"It's obviously working." He held her door open. "As if Seattle could even compare to you, even on a sunny day."

"Just ignore her. That's what I've been doing all morning."

He suspected though that Libby's words contained a grain of truth. He wished he could appease Piper's mind. But right now, they had to hit the road or skip the trip.

"You heard of *Sleepless in Seattle*?" Libby asked. "Well, it was *Sleepless in Cranberry Creek* at our house last night. OMG. Okay, Piper. Sorry, Jake, Alex. I've been trying harder."

"What's OMG?"

How many times would Alex have to correct Jake for saying that now? The hazards of his son hanging out with a teenager.

"Dad, are we going to pass the dinosaurs?" Jake asked, apparently having forgotten about the acronym already. Who knew for how long.

"No, we're going the opposite direction." He glanced at Piper. "We drove through Granger yesterday morning with my dad, a little detour on the way to a job site in West Richland. He had a couple ideas for construction apps, and he was trying to show me how he thought they'd work."

"They have dinosaurs all over there," Jake said. "Even a T. rex and a velociraptor. It was OMG cool."

"Jake! You can't say that!" Libby said before Alex could open his mouth.

"You said it!"

"But I shouldn't. And I apologized. It's...it's like not treating God nice. I just say it because everyone else in my class at school does. But I'm going to try harder to stop. Do you understand?"

"I'll try hard too."

While Libby started an I Spy game with Jake, Alex merged onto Interstate 82 West toward Yakima.

"So what's with security at the Yakima airport?" he asked Piper.

She shook her head. "Tightest security in the nation. Nothing gets by the TSA agents there. They'll confiscate anything that even looks like it should be on the TSA checklist. You won't get four ounces of anything past them. And be careful on I-82. They clock the trees at ten miles an hour around here."

She placed her hand in his when he held his palm up on the console, and pointed to a hawk perched on a pole along the interstate.

"That's an osprey. Rare in the winter, but you do see one occasionally."

So he'd been wrong.

"Which, FYI, is what a sea hawk is. Keep an eye out for hawks and bald eagles too, Jake."

"And don't forget about the magpies," Alex said. He shouldn't tease her, but those common, glorified crows dominated the valley.

"You don't see those on the west side much, I take it?"

"I've not seen a single one there. And know what else I've never seen there? A major highway like this one with so little traffic. In Seattle, I have to gauge traffic before going anywhere inside the city or out. Even with my Emerald City Alternate Route app, which includes back roads and side roads, it's a hassle."

"No kidding," she said. "Any time I'm driving in Seattle, I feel uptight, like I'm dancing on the freeway but can't figure out the rhythm. Like I'll miss my exit because I can't get over or there's a detour. And whose great idea was it to reduce I-5 to two lanes under the convention center?"

Her contented expression when she mentioned the valley and her angst-filled grimace over Seattle traffic reminded him of Libby's earlier statement. Did Piper feel like she had to compete with Seattle? He hoped not.

He was already sold on the valley. That wasn't the problem. She lived here and couldn't leave. He'd never ask her to, at least not as long as she was responsible for Libby.

But making the actual decision to follow his heart and uproot his and Jake's safe routine in the city presented a quandary. If he did it just for Piper, would she see that as a burden? Question it? Worry that if things turned rough with Libby, he'd back out? Or what if Jake made no further progress for months, or longer?

Before making a decision that would change his and Jake's lives entirely, which Alex didn't take lightly, he needed to make certain it was right for him and his son.

But as he drove past vineyards and orchards that followed the path of the Yakima River, as he grabbed the ticket to head into the Yakima Air Terminal parking lot, he knew which way he leaned.

And he couldn't count the times his son had mentioned that Papa and Grandma's and Libby and Piper's homes were larger than the condo.

It wasn't just Piper winning Alex over. The valley offered him and Jake a way of life the city never could. And Alex could neither explain nor deny the progress Jake had made in the weeks they'd stayed in Cranberry Creek, surrounded daily by people who loved him and invested in him, by opportunities to engage with animals and nature and even the weather.

The first thing Jake did every morning was make sure snow still covered the ground. And then he asked when they'd be going over to Piper and Libby's.

Chapter 17

It was pouring rain in Seattle. Of course. Piper tried to tamp down her delight at that fact as she and Libby waited at the Street Bean Coffee Roasters for the guys to return from Alex's staff meeting.

Piper and Libby had already checked in at the Belltown Inn. If the shower would just let up, they'd explore this hip Seattle neighborhood with its shops and trees adorned for the Christmas holidays, though nothing like Cranberry Creek, of course. Blue and clear bulbs ruled the lighting color scheme, enhancing the urban vibe.

To Piper's dismay, she found herself enjoying the urban setting, both in Belltown and the coffeehouse. Young, well-dressed twentysomethings sat with their laptops and tablets against the backdrop of metal and wood grain. Even a pup lay by its owner's feet. A service dog? She'd Googled Street Bean on her phone, and she couldn't help but applaud its efforts to train and work with Seattle's street-involved youths.

As much as Piper hated to admit it, their Uber driver had zipped right into Seattle from Sea-Tac, and they'd beheld the Space Needle through the downpour. Its spire had pumped excitement through her veins and dread in her middle. Seriously, how could Cranberry Creek compete? That structure even inspired her. With that view, she could pull out the pad she kept in her purse and likely sketch out several illustrations for her next project in less than an hour.

“It really should be renamed Misty City,” Libby said as she lifted her mug of almond-milk mocha toward the window and slumped in her chair. “Give me the snow any day. I couldn’t stand this.”

Clearly the vibe and view didn’t entrance Libby as much as it did Piper.

“I hope the guys are done soon. I’m hungry. And they don’t have anything close to a Ding Dong here.”

Alex and Piper had planned to pick up a late lunch at a deli and then head to Jake’s favorite spot, the Olympic Sculpture Park.

All the sweet and savory pastry options offered here, and all Libby could think about were the Ding Dongs that could be bought at any grocery store?

Piper hadn’t taken a swallow of her eggnog macchiato yet She didn’t want to ruin the creamy heart the beanie-capped barista had swirled into it. With a sigh, she brought her cup to her lips.

That was maybe the best sip of coffee *ever*. As much as she loved Java Creek, Piper supposed if she were forced to, she could endure this every day herself. And it wasn’t like Piper hadn’t lived in a large city before—she’d appreciated her five great years in Spokane.

But she hadn’t loved it there, certainly not as much as she’d enjoyed the ranch and her hometown, even with all her heavy responsibilities, since she’d moved back.

As her cup descended toward the table, a bright beam filtered through the large window. Clouds still conquered the sky, but the sun had battled through.

Alex and Jake permeated the beam for a second and then pulled out chairs next to Piper and Libby. In Alex's expensive jeans, brown loafers, and sports coat over his button-down shirt, he looked downright consumable. Jake was dressed almost identically. And while he had purchased several pairs of Carhartts and Dickies for his son, Piper realized Alex hadn't worn anything but his Seattle attire when at the ranch. Minus the suit coat, of course, and plus a leather jacket or Seahawks fleece-lined sweatshirt.

It all added up to yummy either way.

He'd look pretty good in a pair of Wranglers though.

"Your meeting is over already?" Piper asked, glancing at her phone. Only two thirty.

"My partner has everything under control, and I'm not needed to put out any fires. Do you mind?" He pointed to Piper's cup, which at her nod, he lifted. "Didn't I tell you they have the best coffee here?" He grimaced when he set it on the table. "Even with all the froufrou stuff you put in it, it's still not bad."

He lifted the bags he'd set on the table. "Jake and I took the liberty of ordering some sandwiches for you two from the New Town Market. The rain's down to a drizzle, and some sun is poking through. Sorry you girls didn't get to explore more. The hazards of Seattle. Maybe you'll have more of a chance tomorrow."

"I'm not counting on it," Libby said as she slid out of her seat. "Come on, Jake. Let's go see those sculptures."

Jake hopped off his seat and headed toward the door with Libby.

"We're right behind you two," Piper said as she grabbed her purse.

"I know the way," Jake said. "I'm four now. I'll show Wibby where it is."

"I guess we'll just meet you guys there," Libby said with an arched brow their direction.

How did she do that? Piper couldn't lift only one brow, no matter how hard she tried.

Alex stared at the coffeehouse door closing, he on the inside, his mouth half open, and his son on the sidewalk on Third Avenue. Without him.

"It must be a marvel," Piper said. "Let's go get you a cup of real coffee."

"I don't know." Grooves pinched either side of Alex's nose. "Libby's never been here before. The park's not hard to find, but what if Jake..."

"Libby's smart, and she has GPS on her phone. It's been harder for you to let go than you've let on, hasn't it?" She tugged him toward the counter. "You get your coffee, and we'll trail behind them."

He ordered an Americano. He must need something strong.

"Can we see Puget Sound on the walk there?" Piper asked as they made their way to Third Avenue.

"A little bit... It just feels so strange. I've dreamed of moments like this for more than a year," Alex said as he strode onto the sidewalk, Americano in hand. "Now that it's here, I feel more anxious than ever, like the other shoe's about to drop. Or in my case, a little work boot with a flap."

Their fingers entwined as the sun combatted the drizzle, forcing it into submission. The gray sky retreated reluctantly and blue pressed through.

"We might even have perfect views of the Olympics at the park, if the sun stays out," Alex said. "You can't come to

Belltown and miss that view. That'd be a waste of a trip. You can see the mountains from my condo too though, so you'll get another chance after breakfast tomorrow."

After all her anguish over the trip this morning, Piper expected to loathe seeing Alex here. But she didn't. He fit just as well here as he did in Cranberry Creek. The clacking of her bootheels on the sidewalk faded as she slowed Alex to a meander, taking in the mistletoe and garland-draped doorways, the holiday fare on chalkboard menus that waitstaff were setting outside restaurants, the historic structures, the occasional funky artwork on the side of a building, the line of skyscrapers, the people walking their dogs.

The man beside her.

An illustrator would fit right in here, just as she had in Spokane. Her mind painted a watercolor that paired with the tune in her heart, a brush stroke moving upward with the trilling that led to a key change, her mind's and heart's artworks unfinished. She'd figure out the negatives, just as she had in Spokane. It wouldn't happen anytime soon though. She didn't doubt for a second God intended for her to remain in Cranberry Creek and on the ranch as long as she had Libby to care for. Nothing had to be ironed out now. They each had family issues to resolve. They had time. Alex had said more than once he intended to pursue a relationship with her. She wanted to believe his intentions were honorable.

See, she really didn't need Emi and Callie to tell her how to figure herself out.

She would let go of her silly competition with this city and simply relish what time she could spend with this guy without being surrounded by kids, because it wouldn't last long.

Her phone chimed, and she hauled the intruder out of her purse.

And dropped it on the ground.

"Libby's being arrested."

"What? What about Jake? Is she okay? Is he okay? Where are they?" Alex stooped to retrieve her phone. He should have followed those two more closely! Though he'd been more worried about Jake possibly having a meltdown than about Libby finding trouble.

He inhaled deeply twice to calm the hammers pounding in his heart.

Piper stared at him, frozen.

"Can I read her text?" He didn't wait for her nod.

Her phone had already darkened again, so he swiped it. A bench was just ahead of them, and he parked her on it and sat beside her. He didn't dare race off until he knew where the kids were.

He read Libby's message: *At a store near the park. Better get here quick. They might arrest me. Jake's ok.*

He flipped it toward Piper.

"It's terrible, I know." She dropped her head into her palms, her red curls swishing her cheeks.

Okay. So Jake was fine. Libby hadn't been arrested yet and she'd been allowed to text Piper.

But they still didn't know what was going on. If he called her, would she pick up?

He knew which store she must have meant. Belltown Corner Mart. Jake had likely demanded she stop there to get him an apple juice. Alex and Piper were already on Wall near Western

Avenue, about two minutes away. They could get there almost as fast as he could call Libby.

On our way, he texted. *Almost there.* He didn't know if she'd get it.

Piper jumped up just as he'd planned to pull her to her feet.

Uh-oh.

Over her shock now, her forehead crinkling and brows puckering, he could almost see the fireworks ignited by her anger.

She was sizzling mad. Redhead mad!

"Stupid boots!" She jogged alongside him. "And Libby—I could throttle that girl."

He'd set a pace he thought she could keep up with. But even in high heels, she whizzed past him. Did she run marathons in those boots?

The fiery yet sad gaze she leveled on Alex over her shoulder alarmed him more than Libby's text, as if, somehow, she was done. With Libby? With him? Did she plan to shut him out in an attempt to protect him and Jake?

He wouldn't let her. There were things he'd taken care of today she hadn't been privy to. Whatever was going on, he'd support Piper and Libby however he could.

She slowed till he caught up to her. "I guess I don't know where I'm going... I'm so sorry, Alex. I just don't know what gets into her. You and Jake shouldn't have to be exposed to this. Especially Jake."

"I can see her." He pointed straight ahead, to where Libby stood by a storefront, a cop beside her, her hands behind her. Cuffed? Jake leaned casually against the building, clearly unharmed. "Let's not jump to conclusions. Maybe it's a misunderstanding."

"I doubt that! And you don't understand. You know my dad was a police officer for twenty years? Libby has no fear of cops. Just ask our friend Pete, who almost arrested her last time. I'm more worried about the cop than her. She's probably acting belligerent and digging herself in deeper. But I can't believe she'd expose Jake to any of her shenanigans. She really cares about him."

"She wouldn't ever deliberately hurt him." Alex didn't have to think twice about that. "Just hang on till we know what happened."

Fired up, Piper was a raving beauty. Or a revving beauty. Alex would be fine with her everyday alpaca farm prettiness. Or Sunday-best loveliness. *Note to self: stay off her bad side.*

Jake ran toward them. Libby extended an arm to stop him—so she wasn't cuffed—but Jake twisted out of her reach.

"Dad, that man said Wibby stole something. But she didn't. She just walked out of the store with it."

The comment called for a smile even with the dire situation of a police officer with his beefy hand on Libby's arm. Alex towed Jake to him as Piper proceeded with measured steps to the cop and Libby. Piper's hands moved from the back of her head, where she didn't have a ponytail to twirl, to her side, her fingers flexing and relaxing. An attempt to calm herself, Alex guessed. It wasn't his place yet, but he wanted to step in, to be the one who solved this so they could just head to the park with their lunch.

Wait. He'd left the bags with their sandwiches on the bench they'd sat on when the text came in.

This day just kept getting worse. But at least the sun was shining. Funny how the weather didn't reflect the mood at any part of this day.

Alex stood by Piper's side, Jake tucked safely against his legs.

"Hi, Officer." Her voice quavered. "My name is Piper, and Libby is my sister. What happened?"

"I didn't mean to," Libby said, trying to shake off the officer's hand, which didn't budge. "He just wouldn't list—"

"Is her mom around?" The officer, in a ball cap and blue jacket, each with a Seattle Police emblem emblazoned on them, halted Libby's potential torrent with a slight pressure on her arm. His other hand held her pink-leopard-print-covered phone. Did it match her suitcase?

"No, I'm her legal guardian," Piper said.

When her fingers flexed again, Alex wove them with his own, to give her strength.

"I'm Officer Peart. I patrol this area. I happened to be chatting with the clerk inside when I saw your sister walk out of the store with items she did not purchase. Three of them. A soda and an apple juice and a package of Ding Dongs. We take shoplifting seriously here. We've had a rash of petty thefts lately, and we're cracking down."

Piper puffed out a breath as Libby sagged against the storefront.

Alex took a step forward, his hand still linked to Piper's, to prevent passersby from gawking.

Shimmering tears that didn't fall turned the teen's blue orbs into twin dams. Alex willed her to keep them from bursting. At least until they figured out what had happened. But Piper was right. She was behaving more belligerently than shaken up toward the officer. Something else was at play here.

Whatever it was, Alex would stand beside Piper during that crisis too. Any crisis. Anytime.

"Officer, can I hug my sister? And then we can finish this conversation?"

When the officer stepped aside, Piper enfolded Libby, and Alex wrapped one arm around them.

"He seems like a nice guy, Libby," Alex said. "He let you text Piper. That's something."

Libby held Piper's hand, and they faced the officer in a line.

"I let her text when she told me her dad had been on the force for twenty years and had died in the line of duty. Smart kid there, mentioning that." He elevated one side of his mouth. And he didn't move Libby back beside him.

All good signs.

"She says she didn't mean to walk out with the items that she was carrying them and forgot, but my experience with teens tells me that's highly unlikely," the officer said. "Especially since she didn't have enough money to pay for the items."

Libby huddled beside her sister, and though she topped Piper by a good three inches, Piper was the tower here. An impressive tower of strength.

"Why, Libby?" Piper asked.

"I was going to text you to meet me here to pay for the items. I forget to tuck some bills into my phone case this morning. And then...and then... Can my sister see my phone? To read the text just before the one I sent her?" She directed a shaky finger to the officer's hand.

Alex didn't know what the text said, but whatever it was the stark despair in Libby's eyes when she turned her head his way convinced him her distress wasn't related to nearly getting arrested.

Which he confirmed when Piper pressed the phone into his hand and pulled her sister's head down to her shoulder as her body heaved.

This time, he didn't seek permission to read to the text that said it was from Mom's cell.

Great news about the crias. Thanks for texting me last week. But I won't be home for Xmas. Your sis is taking good care of you and the ranch. I'm going to Thailand for a 3 month yoga course. Maybe when I get back. Luv ya.

Chapter 18

Back at the ranch, after a tense drive from Seattle—complete with a two-hour delay on Snoqualmie Pass because of an overturned semitruck and avalanche control—Libby helped Jake out of his car seat. She turned and spoke a quick thank-you to Alex, who placed a palm on her shoulder and said, "Anytime, kid."

Wrong. It would be his last time.

Piper watched as Libby and Jake headed to the barn to check on the crias. Then she swung open the door to Alex's Audi, her decision firm. Semi-firm. Despite the sweet refrain in her heart that had kept playing even after visiting Seattle with Alex—what a disaster that had turned into!—and even though her mind kept painting images of the two of them together. She knew she had to break off any romance with him.

And just when she'd thought she had a handle on things. When she'd believed she had conquered her side of the mountain between them.

Just when she knew she loved him.

The last thing he and his son—especially Jake—needed in their lives was to deal with her and Libby. The two of them encountered and created too much drama. What if it hindered Jake or caused him to revert to panic attacks? The drumstick that had beat that thought continually through Piper's mind since meeting Alex had slammed into a clanging cymbal.

Defected mom. Willful teen. Sister who couldn't provide enough guidance to said teen. Piper couldn't conjure a way to turn that into a hat trick for Alex.

Maybe he should make up his own mind about that. Piper's mental eraser scrubbed away the logic of that whisper.

But it hurt. Saving a man and his son from her dysfunctional family wedged a stake of pain right through her middle. How was it possible that she loved him so much after knowing him only a month? She tilted forward, palms against bent knees nausea churning her stomach.

She heard Alex talking to Callie and Emi on the porch explaining why they'd returned early.

Libby had begged to go home immediately after Piper had explained to Officer Peart about their mom, to show why Libby might have been distressed enough to walk out of the store carrying items she hadn't paid for. He'd said if Libby would apologize to the clerk, he'd let her off with a warning. A contrite Libby, more so than Piper had expected, had delivered her apology.

Alex, great, amazing guy that he was, had ushered them to his condo and piled them into his Audi, saying he'd figure out how to get both vehicles back to Seattle later. He didn't hesitate. He didn't condemn Libby in any way. In fact, he'd hugged her and sympathized, chatting with her and Jake the whole way home

He'd handled it better than Piper had, that was for sure She'd stewed in silence most of the trip, ignoring the Christmas music streaming from SiriusXM.

Piper had expected Libby to act indignant and quarrelsome

down the long 1-90 stretch, but she'd laughed and joked with Jake and Alex. She didn't understand the ramifications of her actions.

But Piper did.

She leaned against the silver Audi's door as Alex hauled her and Libby's carry-ons to the front porch. Snow fell like goose down, escaping through the branches of the chestnut tree, the very tree they'd prayed under, their first prayer together.

True, she hadn't checked with her heavenly Father about this decision.

But she was doing the right thing. Now to take care of it before Callie and Emi barged off the porch into the plumed darkness and tackled her with questions. She wished she could get Alex alone somewhere, but that'd never happen. This was about as close to alone as they'd ever be.

She forced her feet to transport her to the tree and pressed her body against the trunk, its somnolence a quiet consolation. It would still be here after Alex took off with Jake.

The twinkling bulbs and lighted snowmen extended an offer of cheer, but she bolted her eyelashes to her cheeks as footsteps crunched hurriedly her direction.

Alex marched up to her, swooped down, and kissed her startled lips. For the briefest second. Then he caged her in, his hands on either side of her head.

His actions just made this all the harder.

"No."

No? "No what?" *What is he up to?*

"No, you're not ending us over this. Remember—I can read your mind."

She tried to shove him away, but he kept his hands firmly rooted against the tree. She moved to duck under his arms, so he lowered them and clamped her in tighter.

"You might run faster than me, Piper, but Jake and I have been hitting the gym several times a week. He can do several pushups, in case he's never shown you." He bunched his shoulders toward his neck. "Underneath these layers I wear over here to stay warm are muscles strong enough to carry you and the weight on your shoulders. Don't think you can dodge me so easily."

She packaged his forearms with her fingers, intending a last-ditch effort to secure her freedom. But as if coerced by his flexing, her hands skimmed toward his biceps and her thumbs rested on the bulge barely diminished by the blazer.

If only she dared lean on that strength.

"You were silent all the way home. You haven't looked me in the eye since before we left Belltown. You've twirled your hair into ringlets around your head the entire trip. I don't need my mind-meld app to figure out what's going on in that brain of yours."

"I can't expect anyone else to help me with the burden that my family has created."

"Do you consider your sister a burden?"

"No! Mom taking off is not her fault. Sometimes I resent my mother for abandoning her, but that's not what I meant." He wasn't making this easy. Why did her hands on his muscles make her go weak in the knees and lose her resolve? "I meant the burden of my circumstances. Of not knowing if my mother will ever return. I feel overwhelmed by the barriers standing between me and you."

He touched her nose. "The only real barriers between us are our noses." He rubbed hers in an Eskimo kiss.

"Don't take me so lightly!"

"Piper, honey, I'm not." He pulled her to his chest in a

vice grip and then set her back against the tree, his arms fencing her in again. "I get it. I've struggled with the same scenarios. You worry you can't leave. But I know you can't. I've wondered about making life-changing decisions, like moving over here. You think I don't want to or can't handle Libby. And as wonderful as Jake is, I ask myself how you'll ever be able to put up with him so close on our heels for very long. I *get* it, babe."

She shivered despite the warmth of his body. He did get it. But saying it out loud only multiplied the amount dividing them.

"On top of all that, we've only really known each other about a month—"

"Look at me."

Her eyes obeyed his command.

"It's not about time. Trust me. You can know someone for years and not really *know* them. In the time I've known you, I see you love without reservation, to the point of sacrifice. You work hard, and you treat others with kindness and respect." He grinned. "Even Libby, if the situation calls for it."

She tapped her fists against his chest.

"You know what else I know?"

The song in her heart crescendoed. It knew what was coming before her mind could grasp it.

"I know I'd be crazy to not cement things with you right now."

He turned his head when footsteps crunched.

"I shouldn't have put up so many Christmas lights. I can't even tell the girl I love that I love her without an audience of kids!"

"You...you..."

He placed a finger over her lips. "Hold that thought."

He stepped out from under the canopy of branches as Jake rushed toward him, the bottom of his jeans caked in snow, his cheeks ruddy, his hat pulled down around his ears. "Daddy, Mikko and Pikko are so big now! You have to see them. Callie and Emi are in there too."

Piper followed him from her safe spot under the chestnut tree, feeling as if the flush of her cheeks lit up the yard more than the multitude of bulbs.

"What's going on here? Why do you two look so funny?" Libby marched up to Piper. "You're all glowy, and he's all rosy." She tipped her head to the left and then right, closing one eye and squinting the other.

"Your sister is trying to break up with me."

"Because we mess up sometimes? Get over it, Piper. We'll deal with Mom being gone. Just ignore her, Alex. That's what I do when she gets all huffy like this." She flicked her fingers at Piper. "And, Piper. Don't be an idiot. Anyone can see you two are made for each other. Come on, Jake. We'll leave these two lovebirds alone."

She held out her hand, but for the first time, Jake didn't take it. He patted his dad on the leg instead and lifted his heels up and down in jittery excitement.

"Can we say it, Daddy? Now? I kept it secret all day wong!"

"Maybe you should go with Libby—"

"We went to the jew'ry store!"

Libby's and Piper's heads swiveled toward Jake's dad.

Alex groaned and swept the back of a hand to his forehead.

Piper widened her eyes, and she covered her mouth with her palm. Jake couldn't mean...he couldn't possibly have meant... And she'd been about to break up with Alex?

What had Libby called her that day at the Cranberry Creek PD? A buzzkill?

Appropriate.

"To the barn, you two. I'm doing this alone. Semi-alone. And tell Callie and Emi not to interrupt me! Don't tell them why." He aimed a finger at the barn.

Libby towed a chattering Jake back toward the twin crias.

Alex steered Piper over to the wooden fence near the barn, the red and green and blue hues an aura under the downy powder. He swept the snow off the rail, shoved the light strand aside, and perched her there in front of him. He bundled her hands in his.

"Right here, a miracle happened. Jake and I met you and Libby. Under the umbrella of support over here, between you and your sister and my parents, my son has made strides I was beginning to wonder would ever be possible, even with therapy.

"But more than that, my heart attached to yours that very day. I started wondering about lifetime possibilities with you as I left your property. Before that, my heart stirred when you were still on the other side of that wire fence, with Fresca and Dominique."

Piper smiled through her haze of tears, tucked his hands to her chest, and supported her chin on them, not caring that Alex probably felt the thumping that sped up with his every word.

She'd illustrated all kinds of scenarios in her head about how the trip to Seattle would end, but this fence with her on it hadn't been in any of them. Reality was so much more exciting.

"And you!" She smiled. "You captured my heart when you staggered to this fence after Jake went with Libby to see Sophia for the first time." She pinned her gaze on his, completely released from her earlier fretting. She'd been all worked up over…nothing. Nothing they couldn't handle. Together.

"I know there's a lot to work out." He set his forehead against hers. "But I know I don't want to lose you. I don't want me and Jake to lose you and Libby. I don't know all the logistics yet. But I do know we can figure them out. And I know beyond any doubt that you are right for me and Jake.

"On our trip to Seattle the week after the twin crias were born, Jake and I visited a jeweler in Belltown, and we designed a special ring. At the time, Jake didn't realize what it was for but he did today. I can't go talk to your dad, Piper, so I talked to mine last night. And to our heavenly Father. They both gave me the go ahead.

"I want to marry you, if you'll have me. I know you're a package. I am too. But I like packages myself. Especially at Christmas. I love you, Piper. And above all, I want to do this right, honorably. Having kids around will certainly help with that."

He raised her left hand and slid a large diamond on a wide white-gold band onto her ring finger. She blinked at him. Was she dreaming this? She held up the ring to the snowflake-laden sky for confirmation. But wait. Were those…

With his thumb, he tilted her chin. "Yeah. Those cranberry-colored chips between the diamonds on the band were cut and polished from the stones you gathered from the creek. The creek where the Cougar caught the Dawg. Will you marry me, Piper?"

She untangled her other hand from his, and he lifted her from the fence. She wrapped her arms around him and snuggled against his chest, leaning all her weight against him. He didn't budge. Not one inch.

She tipped her head back for his kiss, which lasted deliciously longer than their other ones.

He withdrew and held her brown eyes steady with his hazel ones.

"I almost ruined this moment for us…"

"No, you didn't. I could see the direction of your thoughts, and I wasn't going to let that happen. You didn't ruin anything. You just made it a little more of a challenge to get here."

She trailed a finger through the dimple in his chin. "I trust you to work out the details with me, Alex." She drew air into her lungs, the deepest breath she'd ever inhaled. "I'll marry you. The entire package." She felt as if her heart would strum right out of her chest. She'd found, or rather, God had brought her, the one man who considered her—and her sister—gifts rather than burdens. She felt like shouting *hallelujah* out loud.

But before she could, his head descended again and didn't rise until a voice drifted from the direction of the barn.

"Can we come out yet, Dad?"

The Saturday before Christmas—Christmas at Criations: Kids and Crias

“And over here are Mikko and Pikko. They’re twin babies. We call them *crias*,” Jake said as he escorted a group of children to the pen in the barn where Sophia and her babies stood by the railing. He sifted his fingers through the grain in his baggie and held out a few kibbles to Sophia. “They don’t wike to be touched, so don’t try to pet them.”

Piper watched the scene from her position by the Christmas tree, where she was spreading out ear warmers for the moms along the large diamond-patterned log-cabin tree skirt Piper and Libby’s mom had sewn years ago.

The kids by Jake, in their new hand-knit and hand-crocheted hats, draped themselves over the railing for a better view of Mikko and Pikko. As families had shown up, the children had picked out gift bags from under the tree and traded caps back and forth. The Seahawk-colored lime-and-navy ones were particularly coveted by the teenagers.

“I’m allowed to go in the pen, and I’ll show you how they kiss.” Jake, in his hat Libby had knit and his overalls and work jacket, opened the gate and faced Sophia. He arranged his arms at his sides and bent his knees, and the alpaca dipped her nose to his face.

"Quick, Callie. Take a picture!" he said.

Callie, the event's official photographer and knitting instructor, snapped several photos with her phone. "You just get cuter every day, Jake."

Mikko, who, like his mommy, enjoyed being petted, thrust himself toward Jake. He ignored the baby, as he'd been taught.

"Now wet's go to the paddock," Jake said to the group, "and you can kiss Dominique and Fresca."

The five kids with Jake positioned their arms at their sides and trailed behind him out the open door to the paddock, Callie and several mothers in tow.

This morning as Jake and Libby had decorated the gift bags and attached the cards with hemp string, he'd appointed himself in charge of the barn. Libby had printed dozens of alpaca-themed coloring pages, along with a few Transformer ones at Jake's insistence, and several younger kids sat at a coloring table with fat crayons and markers.

The huge tree in a back corner stood decked to the hilt with clear lights, strand after strand of cranberry beads, silver and cranberry-colored glitter balls, grapevine nesting balls stuffed with coarse alpaca fiber, and white snowflake die-cut ornaments that Libby and Jake had sprinkled with silver glitter. What a mess that had been. Glitter still flashed everywhere in the dining area. Piper cringed every time she walked into the room.

Set in the opposite corner from the tree was the small live band Alex had hired to play Christmas music in the background. Jake had requested "Grandma Got Run Over by a Reindeer" multiple times, until Libby had declared enough.

Despite two inches of fresh snow overnight, about six families and twenty-five kids, ranging in age from four to eighteen, wandered the barn and grounds. Most of the fathers and teen guys hung out at the food tent, which Smokin' Joe's waiters had set up close to the barn, along with two propane fire pits, several tiki torch heaters, and even some minibulbs and garland strung along the tent poles. Visitors dished up hot pulled pork and pulled chicken sandwiches, veggie burgers, coleslaw, and green beans with bacon.

Not exactly Christmas fare, Piper thought as she stood in winter sunshine and dished up a pulled chicken sandwich for herself, but perfect for a ranch event. Libby's dozens of rolled Russian snowballs and snowman sugar cookies with frosting and sprinkles made up for that. Piper stacked two of each onto her plate and headed back to the barn.

Libby stood at the waist-high skirting table, a chicken-wire mesh strung between old fence railings that their father had made. She would show the women how they separated the course fiber from the soft. She unrolled rose-gray fleece bound for the Spring Harvest Fiber Mill in Sunnyside, where it would be spun into yarn. She slid the paper casing from beneath the fiber and tossed it to the floor. After spreading the fiber out, she tore some lengths from the middle and had the group feel its softness. She split a piece off an edge and noted its coarseness before dropping it to the cement floor too, where other fiber lay under and surrounding the table.

As she pitched another piece to the ground, Jake moved his group toward her.

He reached into a basket next to the skirting table and picked up a softball-sized grapevine ball. He bent and scooped up several of the coarse fiber strands Libby had discarded. "You can use the fluffy stuff on the floor," he said to his audience. "You stuff it into this ball and hang it on a tree so birds can make a nest from it."

And Alex...was nowhere to be found.

Libby walked up to Piper, who leaned her back against the wall by the Christmas tree.

"Well, big sister, you got your Christmas event," Libby said as she brushed her palms along her jeans. She'd at least jazzed up today's outfit with a red Santa hat with a string of battery-operated minibulbs around the top of the white brim.

"Not just me. You too. But it really isn't about us, is it?"

Piper's gaze traveled around the barn, to the children pointing to the twin crias, to the moms sitting at Callie's yarn table and exploring knitting needles and yarns, to the handsome devil of a guy—apparently a brother of one of the dads—who tracked Callie's every movement, to the kids filling nesting balls. Emi had intended to make an appearance, but an emergency call from a goat farm in Prosser had called her out of town.

"Can you believe Jake?" Libby asked as she tipped a shoulder against the wall. "He acts like he was born and raised here, the little know-it-all. And do you think Callie even notices that guy who can't take his eyes off her?" Her hand drifted toward a cookie on Piper's plate.

"Get your dirty hand away from my cookie." Piper shoved it away. "Go wash at the sink if you want to eat."

"Just drop one snowball cookie into my mouth then." Libby tilted forward and opened her mouth.

Piper popped one in, the sparkle of the diamond and contraband Cranberry Creek stones of her engagement ring reminding her how glad she was to be left handed—more opportunities to notice the ring without being so obvious.

"He does seem to be doing great, don't you think?" Libby asked after she swallowed the cookie. "He hasn't asked about Alex at all."

Earlier, Alex had tried to take Jake with him to run to his parents' cabin. He'd left his laptop behind, and his business partner had called. Jake had insisted he couldn't leave Mikko and Pikko, that Brisco could go with his dad instead.

Alex had started to protest, but Libby had kicked him politely in the shin and told him to listen to his son.

Jake had retrieved Brisco from the south pasture, where he guarded the young families, and a bemused and dazed Alex had loaded the Great Pyrenees into his pickup and drove off the ranch, completely Jake-free for the first time in over a year.

Piper figured she and Jake's father would have quite a bit to talk about later.

"That poor guy doesn't stand a chance with Callie, does he?" Libby asked as the band started its country rendition of "The First Noel."

"Not likely." Piper placed her chilled hands under her bottom, palms against the wall, and pressed against them. "She's going to be a tough one to crack. After everything she's been through, I can't picture her ever trusting a man enough to allow him to get close to her. It'll take a special guy with character and faith and determination, because Callie will try to run him off in short order."

"She likes Alex."

"Yeah, he'd be the exception, but, well..." She moved her left hand from behind her and paraded her ring in front of Libby. "And after today, we're getting closer to our dream of a kid-free date."

Libby shoulder-bumped her. "We're not that bad. I do my

best to keep Jake distracted so you two can have a conversation without 'Dad' this and 'Piper' that."

Piper struggled to clear the emotion clogging her throat. "You're awesome with him, Libby."

"Aww, don't get all mushy. He's a great kid. I love him."

Piper could only nod, her throat and chest so tight, no words could pass.

Libby shifted from foot to foot. Drummed her fingers on the wall.

"It's Christmas in two days," she said, wrapping her arms around her middle. "I'm not going to get my wish, am I?"

Piper tugged her close. "No, baby, you're not."

She spotted Alex entering the barn. He strode straight to his son, who lifted his nesting ball for Alex's examination.

"But it's all right, isn't it?" Libby said into Piper's hair. "I've got you and Alex and Jake, and even Alex's parents. They already act like I'm part of their family. Like I'm a niece or something. It's kind of sweet."

They'd had an engagement celebration dinner with Alex's parents Thursday night. The couple had welcomed Libby and Piper with enthusiasm and already had Christmas presents for them under their tree and a stocking for Libby, right next to Jake's, on the fireplace mantel.

"Yep, we'll be all right, Libby." The band struck up "Joy to the World" in the background, and Piper eased her sister out of her arms as Alex, holding Jake's hand, trekked their way.

"I miss Mom, and Dad too. But it's still going to be a wonderful Christmas, isn't it?"

"One of our best," Piper said as she stepped into Alex's hug. "It's a God thing."

Hallelujah Hat

Pattern by Dori Harrell

Don't you just love Piper's hat? I do too, so I thought, why not design it for my readers who knit? And I did! I've tested the pattern. It's not identical, but it's close, and it looks great, with and without a pom-pom. But should you notice an error, please contact me (dori@doriharrell.com), and I'll update and send you the new file in a PDF format. Send me photos of you in your hat! I'll post them on my website (doriharrell.com).

Note

For this pattern, you will be placing markers and decreasing between one set and increasing between the other set for the first part of the crown. I recommend using different-color markers for the decreasing set and the increasing set, as well as a third color for the marker that begins the round. For the purpose of this pattern, I used *green* as the decreasing set and *purple* as the increasing set. The joining marker is red. You, of course, may use any colors you prefer.

Supplies

3.5 oz (104 yards) bulky weight alpaca blend yarn (I used Snuggle). That amount will knit up one hat, but an additional amount may be needed for a pom-pom.

Size 8 circular needle (16 in.)

Size 10 circular needle (16 in.)

5 size 10 dpns

8 green markers (or your color preference)

8 purple markers (or your color preference)

1 red marker (or your color preference)—joining marker

Glossary of Terms Used

co—cast on

dec—decrease

dpn(s)—double-pointed needle(s)

in.—inch

inc—increase

k—knit

k2tog—knit 2 together (left-leaning decrease)

m1L—make 1 left (left-leaning increase)—Pick up bar between the stitch you just knit and the one you're about to knit, bringing needle from front to back. Knit into the back of the new stitch.

m1R—make 1 right (right-leaning increase)—Pick up bar between the stitch you just knit and the one you're about to knit, bringing the needle from back to front Knit into the front of the new stich. Here's a great link with a videos for m1L and m1R: https://www.purlsoho com/create/make-one-right-m1r-make-one-left-m1l/

pm—place marker

p—purl

rm—remove marker

sm—slip marker

ssk—slip, slip, knit (right-leaning decrease)

sts—stitches

Ribbing

On size 8 circular needle (16 in.), CO 74 sts.

Place red marker. Join, being sure sts are not twisted.

K1, p1 for 2 in. (2.5 in or 3 in. if you prefer a wider brim. I did my ribbing to 3 in., as I like to fold mine up a bit sometimes.)

Crown

Switch to size 10 needles. You will place markers on the first round. In addition, **dec 2 sts evenly on the first round**, making sure you have the appropriate number of sts between markers.

R 1: (dec 2 sts evenly) k1, pm (green), k10, pm (green), k3, pm (purple), k2, pm (purple), K3, pm (green), k10, pm (green), k3, pm (purple), k2, pm (purple), k3, pm (green), k10, pm (green), k3, pm (purple), k2, pm (purple), k3, pm (green), k10, pm (green), k3, pm (purple), k2, pm (purple), k2. (72 sts on needle.)

R 2: k1, sm, p10, sm, k1, p1, k1, sm, p2, sm, k1, p1, k1, sm, p10, sm, k1, p1, k1, sm, p2, sm, k1, p1, k1, sm, p10, sm, k1, p1, k1, sm, p2, sm, k1, p1, k1, sm, p10, sm, k1, p1, k1, sm, p2, sm, k1, p1.

R 3: k1, sm, k10, sm, k3, sm, k2, sm, K3, sm, k10, sm, k3, sm, k2, sm, k3, sm, k10, sm, k3, sm, k2, sm, k3, sm, k10, sm, k3, sm, k2, sm, k2.

R 4: k1, sm, p10, sm, k1, p1, k1, sm, p2, sm, k1, p1, k1, sm, p10, sm, k1, p1, k1, sm, p2, sm, k1, p1, k1, sm, p10, sm, k1, p1, k1, sm, p2, sm, k1, p1, k1, sm, p10, sm, k1, p1, k1, sm, p2, sm, k1, p1.

Begin decreases and increases between markers

R 1: k1, sm, k2tog, k to within 2 sts of next marker, ssk, sm, k3, sm, m1R, k to within 1 st of next marker, m1L k1, sm, k3, sm, k2tog, k to within 2 sts of next marker, ssk, sm, k3, sm, m1R, k to within 1 st of next marker, m1L k1, sm, k3, sm, k2tog, k to within 2 sts of next marker, ssk, sm, k3, sm, m1R, k to within 1 st of next marker, m1L k1, sm, k3, sm, k2tog, k to within 2 sts of next marker, ssk, sm, k3, sm, m1R, k to within 1 st of next marker, m1L k1, k2. (You now have 8 sts between green markers and 4 sts between purple markers.)

R 2: k1, sm, purl sts between green markers, sm, k1, p1 k1, sm, purl sts between purple markers, sm, k1, p1 k1, sm, purl sts between green markers, k1, p1, k1, sm purl sts between purple markers, sm, k1, p1, p1, purl sts between green markers, k1, p1, k1, sm, purl sts between purple markers, sm, k1, p1, k1, purl sts between green markers, sm, k1, p1, k1, sm, purl sts between purple markers, k1, p1.

Repeat rounds **1 and 2**, maintaining established increase and decreases. Continue in pattern until you have 2 sts between the green markers and 10 sts between the purple markers. (You still have 72 sts on your needles).

Then knit even in established pattern, **but with no decreases or increases between markers**, until piece measures 7 in. from bottom.

Begin crown decreases

R 1: k1, sm, k the 2 sts between green markers, sm, k3, sm, k2tog, k to within 2 sts of next marker, ssk, sm, k3, sm, k sts between green markers, sm, k3, sm, k2tog, k to within 2 sts of next marker, ssk, sm, k3, sm, k sts between green markers, sm, k3, sm, k2tog, k to within 2 sts of next marker, ssk, sm, k3, sm, k sts between green markers, sm, k3, sm, k2tog, k to within 2 sts of next marker, ssk, sm, k2.

R 2: R 4: k1, sm, purl sts between green markers, sm, k1, p1, k1, sm, purl sts between purple markers, sm, k1, p1, k1, sm, purl sts between green markers, sm, k1, p1, k1, sm, purl sts between purple markers, sm, k1, p1, p1, sm, purl sts between green markers, k1, p1, k1, sm, purl sts between purple markers, sm, k1, p1, k1, sm, purl sts between green markers, sm, k1, p1, k1, sm, purl sts between purple markers, k1, p1.

Repeat rounds **1 and 2** until you have 2 sts between the purple markers. (There are now 2 sts between the green markers and 2 sts between the purple markers).

Begin new rounds of decreases

R 1: k1, sm, k2tog between green markers, sm, k3, sm, k2tog between purple markers, sm, k3, sm, k2tog between green markers, sm, k3, sm, k2tog between purple markers, k3, sm, k3, sm, k2tog between green markers, k3, k2tog between purple markers, sm, k3, sm, k2tog between purple markers, sm, k3, sm, k2tog between green markers, sm, k3, sm, k2tog between purple markers, k2.

R 2: (remove markers [rm] as you go around, except for the red joining marker) k1, rm, p1, rm, k1, p1, k1, rm, p1, rm, k1, p1, k1, rm, p1, rm, k1, p1, k1, rm, p1, rm, k1, p1, k1, rm, p1, rm, k1, p1, k1, rm, k1, p1, k1, rm, p1, rm, k1, p1, k1, rm, p1, rm, k1, p1.

R 3: (switch to dpns, distributing 5 sts across 4 needles) k2tog, k1, ssk, k1, k2tog, k1, ssk, k1, k2tog, k1, ssk, k1, k2tog, k1, ssk, k1, k2tog, k1, ssk, k2tog. (20 sts.)

R 4: Using spare needle, *k2tog, p1, k2tog.* Repeat between asterisks on remaining 3 needles. (12 sts.)

R 5: *k2tog, k1.* Repeat between asterisks on remaining 3 needles. (8 sts.)

Finishing

Cut yarn, leaving a long tail. Weave tail through remaining sts and pull tight. Weave in ends on wrong side.

Make or buy large pom-pom and sew on. (It looks great without a pom-pom too!)

About the Author

Dori Harrell is a multiple award-winning writer, and she reads more books than anyone she knows. Of course, the fact that she's a full-time book editor provides her plenty of reading material.

Dori grew up on the rainy west side of the Cascade Mountains in Washington State, in the Seattle area, and she graduated from the University of Washington with a double major in journalism and political science. She crossed over to the sunny, arid east side of the Cascades when she married her husband, Doug. Dori is an avid runner and knitter and loves to camp, fish, hike, and watch Seahawks games (go Hawks!). She has an amazing family and wonderful friends. Dori is a huge fan of the Pacific Northwest and cannot imagine living anywhere else.

She and Doug have four grown children, and they don't get to see their seven grandchildren nearly enough.

Look for book 2 in the Cranberry Creek series in spring 2018.

If you enjoyed *A Christmas Hallelujah*, Dori would love to hear from you and to connect with you!

Through her reader group: http://eepurl.com/c5vCLn

On her website: http://www.doriharrell.com

On Facebook: https://www.facebook.com/Dori-Harrell-497759770599706/

Made in the USA
Columbia, SC
16 November 2017